Finally
COOPER

Stacey Matson

Scholastic Canada Ltd.
Toronto New York London Auckland Sydney
Mexico City New Delhi Hong Kong Buenos Aires

Scholastic Canada Ltd.
604 King Street West, Toronto, Ontario M5V 1E1, Canada

Scholastic Inc.
557 Broadway, New York, NY 10012, USA

Scholastic Australia Pty Limited
PO Box 579, Gosford, NSW 2250, Australia

Scholastic New Zealand Limited
Private Bag 94407, Botany, Manukau 2163, New Zealand

Scholastic Children's Books
Euston House, 24 Eversholt Street, London NW1 1DB, UK

www.scholastic.ca

Library and Archives Canada Cataloguing in Publication

Title: Finding Cooper / Stacey Matson.

Names: Matson, Stacey, author.

Identifiers: Canadiana (print) 20190098228 | Canadiana (ebook)
20190098236 | ISBN 9781443163415

(softcover) | ISBN 9781443163422 (ebook)

Subjects: LCSH: Cooper, D. B—Juvenile fiction.

Classification: LCC PS8626.A839 F55 2019 | DDC jC813/.6—dc23

Photos © Shutterstock: cover left (Viorel Sima), cover center right,
iii (Pikovit), cover bottom right (Stanislaw Mikulski), 1 stamp and
throughout (carmen2011).

Text copyright © 2019 by Stacey Matson.

6 5 4 3 2 1   Printed in Canada 139   19 20 21 22 23

For Courtney
in Courtenay

CHAPTER 1

CASE: 0023 / FILE: 0012
LOCATION: Kelowna, British Columbia
STATUS: Unsolved

With great regret I acknowledge that Case File 0023-0012, aka "The Lake Disturbance," aka "Monster from the Deep," remains unsolved. After spending the last two weeks of August in the Okanagan Valley, I, Agent Cooper Arcano, uncovered no solid evidence of the great lake creature commonly known as Ogopogo despite exhaustive research. I ensured that each afternoon included intense stakeouts of the lake from various beach access points around Kelowna and the surrounding area.

Special Agents Dawn Cooke-Arcano and Marco Arcano, aka the "Parental Unit," were not helpful in lake observations, as they spent most afternoons asleep (Agent Marco Arcano) or involved in independent research that included prolific reading of romance novels (Agent Dawn Cooke-Arcano). However, their ability to drive a car was helpful in navigating Okanagan Lake.

There was one incident of note while driving to find our cabin. I have transcribed the dialogue as I remember it; however, it has been redacted for improper language use. The day was August 24; the time was 13:08.

AGENT DAWN: The GPS says you have to turn left.

AGENT MARCO: There is no left. There's a ████ lake on the left.

AGENT DAWN: Well, the GPS says . . .

AGENT COOPER: Hey! I think I saw something!

AGENT MARCO: Was it a boat launch? Your mother seems to think that our car magically turns into a boat.

AGENT COOPER: There's something in the lake! I think I see Ogopogo in the lake!

AGENT COOPER: There! Guys! Do you see it? Look through the trees!

AGENT COOPER: See? There's a dark thing in the water. I think he's out there!

AGENT DAWN: That's nice, honey. Wouldn't that be exciting?

AGENT COOPER: Mom! Look! Did you see it? Dad! Can we stop for a second?

AGENT DAWN: Ha! Turn left! Like I said! Victory is mine!

AGENT COOPER: Dad! Stop!

AGENT MARCO: Buddy, there's nowhere to pull off.

AGENT COOPER: Pull way over onto the gravel.
Please?

AGENT DAWN: Honey, we can't. Your dad is too busy
being wrong.

AGENT COOPER: I can't see anything anymore.

That was the only possible sighting of Ogopogo.
By the time we reached our final destination, the
lake was calm. Further observation that day was
hampered by the fact that the sun was setting, and
that Dana Scully ran off without her leash, which
required me to chase her along the shoreline
for thirty minutes. Please note: This is not the
original Agent Dana Scully from *The X-Files*. This
is Dana Scully, newly rescued Canine Companion
to Agent Cooper. She will eventually be trained
to sniff out monsters but is currently working on
coming when called and returning the ball during
fetch, not just looking at it and barking.

END MISSIVE

The first thing I did when we got home from vacation was call my best friend, Ali.

"Dude! Did you find the Loch Ness?" he asked
excitedly. Ali shares my love of unsolved mysteries,
although he definitely doesn't have the same drive
to solve them.

"You mean Ogopogo? No. I mean, I might have
seen something, but Dad wouldn't stop to find out."

"Lame. Maybe next time."

"Yeah. Hopefully. How was soccer camp?" I
asked. I didn't like soccer, but Ali loved it.

"Oh man. So awesome. I scored two goals for my cabin in the championship game. I was a soccer god."

"Thor of the Field," I announced in a deep voice.

"Oh, that reminds me of a joke. Why is Iron Man so good at soccer?" Ali asked.

"Uh . . ."

"Because he's Iron Man!"

I laughed. "That's so stupid."

"I know. But you laughed. Oh, hey, do you remember Tristan? He's coming to our school this year. Won't that be awesome?"

Tristan Khoury was on Ali's soccer team. I'd met him a couple of times at Ali's games, but we didn't hang out. He was okay, I guess, but all he talked about was soccer and video games. He was one of those guys that everyone likes. I didn't get the appeal, but Ali would talk about how cool he was after practice and stuff. Tristan was okay, but I didn't really want him to be at my school.

I paused for a second, then lied. "I don't really remember him. Is he the guy who had the purple cleats?"

"Totally, that's him. He's hilarious! Oh man. This year is going to be the best."

"For sure," I mumbled, trying to sound like I meant it.

"Hey, how were your parents?" Ali's voice dropped to a whisper, even though we were on the phone and only I could hear him.

I looked around. Dad was out in the garage and Mom was in the laundry room.

I lowered my voice too. "Lame. They argued about everything, and we weren't ever allowed to eat out, even though the place we stayed was right next to the Burger Shack and it smelled like fries all the time."

"Oh man. That sucks. You wanna sleep over? Last Saturday before school starts. I got a couple new comics. And my mom bought fries at the store today, so you don't have to suffer any longer."

"Definitely. Let me ask." I covered the phone with my hand and shouted downstairs. "MOM! CAN I SLEEP OVER AT ALI'S?!"

There was no response. I turned back to the phone. "Hold on." I ran downstairs two at a time. "Can I sleep over at Ali's tonight?"

"We just got home."

"So?"

"So . . . it's just . . ." Mom stumbled for a reason. "Okay, fine. But we'll be going straight to see Grandpa tomorrow when I pick you up, so don't stay up all night. I don't want to deal with a grumpy kid."

"I won't be grumpy," I promised. If anyone was grumpy these days, it was Mom, but I didn't say that part. "Thanks," I added. She nodded and went back to unpacking and sorting dirty clothes.

"Ali? I'm in," I said. "See you soon!"

That night I finally got some french fries that Mrs. Singh made, and we read through Ali's new comics.

We love comics, but Ali definitely loves them more. We're even working on drawing our own series. It's about a superhero named the American Marmot, who has radioactive spit and a high-pitched whistle that can break eardrums. We worked on a new storyline where the American Marmot has to fight Ogopogo, and Ali talked about all the things that happened at soccer camp. Every story had Tristan in it. I hoped Tristan knew that Ali was my best friend, and not his. We had been friends since kindergarten.

The best part of sleeping over at Ali's is that his parents let us sleep in front of the TV and watch full episodes of *The X-Files*. We love *The X-Files*, even though it was on a really long time ago. Plus, I'm not allowed to watch it at home because my parents think it's "too mature." So it's extra cool to get to watch it and not have my parents know.

The X-Files originally had *nine* seasons of unsolved mysteries. I know it's supposedly fiction, but where did they get their inspiration from? I bet at least ninety percent of their shows were based on real stories. Like they said at the beginning of the show, The Truth Is Out There. And Ali and I are pretty sure we are going to find it. I really want to be like Fox Mulder, one of the main characters (the other is Dana Scully, who I named my dog after, because even though she's super cool, Ali didn't want to be nicknamed Scully). Mulder and Scully are FBI agents who specialize in paranormal mysteries.

We watched the episode where Mulder and Scully investigate a lake monster called Big Blue. Then we made a comic where the American Marmot fights a lake monster named Logo Mess, who is covered in brand logos and is angry that she can't be ad-free like all the other lake monsters. We ended up staying up pretty late, so I was kind of exhausted when Mom came to pick me up the next morning.

When I got in the car, Mom looked at me and shook her head. "Look at those bags under your eyes. I told you to go to bed early. We have to get your school supplies today too."

I knew she would be the grumpy one, not me. I was actually in a pretty good mood. We hadn't seen Grandpa since before our vacation. I used to love seeing Grandpa. He was never big on talking, but every time I saw him he would give me an American dollar bill. He would make a big show of taking out his wallet and rifling through it until he pulled out the dollar. Then he would hand it to me and say, "In case of emergencies, Cooper." And I would nod and put it in my pocket. I kept all of them in a special lockbox he gave me for Christmas one year. Plus, he loved ice cream, so we always got ice cream when we went to Ladner to visit him. He and I both got cookies and cream every time.

These days, though, Grandpa was turning into a different person.

CHAPTER 2

Grandpa lives in a fancy hospital. It's not actually a hospital. It's called "Golden Sunsets Care Home." I think that's supposed to make it sound warm and cozy. It's kind of the opposite of that.

For one thing, it's in the Ladner suburbs, so I don't think anyone there can even see the sunset. It's only a few storeys high and it's surrounded by apartment buildings. The most annoying thing is how long it takes us to get there. Ladner is at least a forty-five-minute drive from our house in Vancouver. Also, as a detective, I would suspect some foul play, because everyone who lives there seems to be totally out of it.

There are a few different areas in Golden Sunsets. Grandpa lives in the creepiest part. His ward is a lockdown ward. The door is always locked from the outside *and* the inside. The first time we went to see him after they'd moved him into the Alzheimer's ward, I thought it was kind of cool. We were like spies who had to know the four-digit passcode to get through the door. Now I know better. There's nothing spy-like about it.

The area is okay, but it smells like pee and bleach, and there are old people just shuffling around or sitting blankly in front of a TV or a table. Sometimes there's shouting happening, and then the nurses walk by super fast toward the noise. Those are the worst moments. And I know it's not just me who feels that way. Mom will sometimes take my hand and not let go, even if I try to pull away. (I pull away because I'm not an idiot. No almost-thirteen-year-old holds his mom's hand in public, even in front of old people.)

It's really no wonder that in Season Two of *The X-Files* there's an episode that takes place in an old folks' home. If I was younger, I would have nightmares about visiting Golden Sunsets.

I didn't think Grandpa needed to be in the ward for people with dementia and Alzheimer's. It seemed like he remembered all the important stuff, like my name and that he should give me a dollar. From what I heard about Alzheimer's disease, I assumed he would be putting pants on his head as a hat or something, but nothing that funny ever happens. He just forgets what certain things are called, or repeats conversations a billion times. But the last time we went, before going on summer vacation, he couldn't remember who my dad was at first, and he didn't know who Ali was when I talked about him, which was weird, because he's met him a ton.

Mom warned me on the way in that he may be worse than when we saw him three weeks ago, but I wasn't worried. If anything, I had my tablet in my backpack, so I could play games while he and Mom talked.

Grandpa's room has only one chair in it, so we sat at one of the "chatting stations," as my mom calls them. They are in the common area, the first room you walk into after passing the door of doom. There are tables with kids' jigsaw puzzles on them, a couple of armchairs in little groups around the windows, and then a few chairs pointed at the large TV mounted high on the wall.

When we got there, I lounged in one of the armchairs and let Mom go and get Grandpa. I opened my tablet so I could finish reading this thing I'd found on the Alert Bay Sasquatch recordings. It always took way longer than I thought it would for Mom and Grandpa to come to the common room.

I heard Mom talking as they came down the hall. There's never a lot of people talking, so any conversation echoes in that place, but Mom also speaks really loudly to Grandpa even though he isn't deaf at all.

"And I brought your grandson, Cooper. He's here too," I heard Mom say. I put my tablet beside me on the chair and stood up as they entered.

"Hey, Grandpa!" I moved in to give him a hug. He stood kind of limply, not returning the squeeze. I looked up at him and smiled expectantly.

"Hello," he said hesitantly. "What's your name?"

"Cooper." I repeated what Mom had just said. How come he didn't know my name? He was the one who named me. At least, that's what I'd always been told, by him and by my mom.

"Sorry. Right. Cooper. Sorry," he said distractedly.

He didn't seem to be okay at all today. I looked at Mom, and she shook her head from side to side. I didn't know what that meant either.

I tried again. "How's it going, Grandpa? Got anything for me?"

"Cooper!" Mom scolded.

Grandpa looked confused, so I explained. "It's just that you normally have a dollar bill for me. In your wallet."

"Cooper Arcano!" Mom seemed embarrassed by my asking, but I didn't mind. If he didn't remember, that was okay. I just thought he should be reminded of it. I didn't want him to feel bad if he remembered after we left.

"Oh, oh. Um . . ." Grandpa reached and pulled his wallet from his back pocket. When he did, a few pieces of paper fluttered to the ground. I bent down to pick them up. One was an old receipt, but the other was a piece of paper that had been folded and unfolded so many times the creases were ripping. I read it quickly. It said: "Linda: Wife. Dead / Dawn: Daughter. Married to Marco / Jane: Daughter. Lives in Toronto, ON / Cooper: Grandson. Dawn's son."

He carried around a list of his family members? Something about seeing that made me feel sad, so I handed it back quickly.

"Don't worry about it, Grandpa," I said.

"No, no. You want money," he said, handing me an American five-dollar bill. I smiled grandly. Every other time he only ever gave me a dollar bill.

"Sweet! Thanks, Grandpa!" I said, ignoring the look on my mother's face. She was clearly unimpressed.

We all sat down, our chairs forming a small triangle. Mom started to tell Grandpa about our trip to the Okanagan, so I turned back to my tablet to keep reading.

"What's he doing?" he asked Mom, as though I wasn't there.

"Cooper . . ." Mom paused to emphasize my name. "Cooper, your grandson, is playing a game on his tablet. It's a hand-held computer." She gestured at me. "Show Grandpa your tablet."

I flashed the screen in his direction. "See? And I'm not playing a game. It's got the internet, so I can look stuff up," I said.

Grandpa repeated my name a few times under his breath. "Cooper . . . Cooper." It was like he was trying to memorize it. "What stuff?" he asked. "What kind of stuff do you look up?"

"Anything I want," I said. "The internet has everything."

"Dad, you remember when we set up that email

address for you? Do you remember writing emails? That used the internet too," Mom explained.

"I would never touch a thing like that," Grandpa said. "That's how kids get fat, spending all day on things like that."

"You'll be pleased to know that Cooper is starting grade seven on Tuesday, Dad. He's in the science enrichment program!" Mom tried to change the subject.

"When you say everything—" Grandpa was looking at me. "—do you mean everything? Cooper?"

"Yeah, sure," I said. "What do you want to know?"

"The internet is great, Dad! I learned how to properly fold fitted sheets. Do you remember how Mom used to get so mad that I didn't know how to fold a fitted sheet?" Mom forced a laugh.

"Does it tell you who D.B. Cooper was?" Grandpa asked.

"I'm Cooper, Grandpa," I said. Now I was confused.

"Not you. You're not D.B. Cooper. Does it tell you who D.B. Cooper was?" He seemed to be getting worked up, but I didn't know what he was talking about.

"Probably," I said. "Cooper is a pretty common name. I bet there are lots of Coopers. None as good as me, though," I added.

"It can't. It can't tell you!" He raised his voice. One of the nurses looked over in our direction.

"Dad, he's joking. It doesn't tell you who C.B. Cooper is," Mom soothed.

"D.B.!! DEE! BEE!" Grandpa was yelling full out now.

"Honey, tell him you were joking. There's nothing about D.B. Cooper. Dad, I promise there's no reason to get upset!" Mom was talking loudly now, and the nurse was on her way to check on us. Mom put her hand on my shoulder and pressed hard to make her point. I got it.

"Grandpa, I was joking. D.B. Cooper is nowhere on the internet," I said.

"Is everything okay over here, Mr. Cooke?" The nurse spoke to Grandpa but was looking at Mom the whole time.

"There's nothing on there?" Grandpa pointed at my tablet.

"Nothing," I said. I turned the screen off and flashed it over so he could see that it was dark.

He looked relieved and defeated at the same time. "I'm tired. I want to go to bed."

"That's probably a good idea, Dad. A nap is always nice. We will be back next week, okay?"

Mom helped Grandpa stand up from the low chair and kissed him on the cheek.

"Say goodbye to your grandfather," she ordered.

"Bye, Grandpa," I said. She gestured at Grandpa, so I moved in and wrapped one arm around him, awkwardly giving him a half hug. He pulled away from me and started walking to his room.

14

"Bye, Dad. I love you," Mom called after him. He waved over his shoulder and kept walking with the nurse.

Mom looked over at me with an expression I couldn't read. "Ready to go home?" she asked.

"Ready for school supplies, you mean?"

She sighed. "Right. Let's go, then."

It wasn't until we were in the store that either of us spoke again.

"Can I get these pencil crayons?" I pointed to a fancy metal case. There were a hundred colours. They would be amazing for my and Ali's comics.

"We don't have that kind of money. You don't need them."

"I kind of do, Mom. Ali and I need them."

"We can get a pack of sixteen at the dollar store. You don't need those ones."

I scowled at her. How could a set of pencil crayons be too expensive? They were necessary. I wished we had come here before seeing Grandpa. Mom would have been in a better mood. Then I thought about Grandpa's freak-out.

"Mom, who is D.B. Cooper?"

"Honestly, Cooper. I don't know. I doubt it's anyone. Can you choose a pencil case that is under five dollars, and quickly please? I have a headache."

I pulled a blue case from the bottom shelf and dropped it in the basket.

"If it's no one, why did Grandpa freak out?"

"I don't know. With Alzheimer's he can get

suddenly confused or angry. Like he did today. Grandpa's memory is kind of like Swiss cheese right now. There are all kinds of holes. I don't know. It's frustrating," She looked at the list she had. "Let's get a pack of binder dividers and then we're done. I'm ready to go home. And I bet your dad didn't make dinner or turn the laundry over."

Mom was usually in a terrible mood after visiting Grandpa. It hadn't always been like this, but since he got moved into the Alzheimer's ward, she was getting worse. She took it out on me by nagging me about too much TV or screen time. It was annoying.

Worse, though, were the fights she had with my dad. I would listen to them bicker over the tiniest things, like how to load the dishwasher, or how Dad left glasses all over the house. And then he would bite back with comments about whatever she was doing to be annoying too. The worst part of visiting Grandpa was going home after.

CHAPTER 3

CASE: 0024 / FILE: 0001
LOCATION: Vancouver, British Columbia
STATUS: Pending

Agent Cooper Arcano will be taking the lead on the newest unsolved mystery, to be commonly known as "The Cooper File."

The facts surrounding this case are still unclear. Here is a transcript of the initial information gathering, taken at the dinner table Sunday evening.

AGENT MARCO: How was Grandpa today?

AGENT COOPER: Weird.

AGENT DAWN: He was . . . off.

AGENT COOPER: Also known as weird.

AGENT MARCO: Weirder-than-normal weird?

AGENT COOPER: He was freaking out about some guy not being on the internet . . .

AGENT DAWN: Don't talk with your mouth full. Not freaking out. Just . . . distressed.

AGENT COOPER: Cooper someone. Or someone Cooper?

AGENT DAWN: D.B. Cooper.

AGENT MARCO: D.B. Cooper? The hijacker who jumped out of the plane? That was years ago!

AGENT COOPER: Is that who he is? He hijacked a plane?

AGENT DAWN: Chew with your mouth closed, please.

AGENT COOPER: This is gross?

AGENT MARCO: Not as gross as this!

AGENT DAWN: Marco. Don't encourage him. Is it too much to ask you both to have table manners?

AGENT MARCO: Oh, pip, pip. I didn't realize we were expecting the Queen for dinner.

AGENT COOPER: Dad, did you know D.B. Cooper? Is he a real person?

AGENT MARCO: I think he died or something. I don't really remember the whole story.

AGENT COOPER: But he was real?

AGENT MARCO: Yeah. Look him up after supper. It's kind of a cool . . . Dana Scully! GET DOWN!

Information gathering was interrupted when Dana Scully jumped up onto the table and tried to eat Agent Marco's chicken. After supper, more in-depth research happened on the internet, and it turns out D.B. Cooper *was* a real person. Agent Marco's initial information was proven correct.

Here are the key facts of the D.B. Cooper case:

1) D.B. Cooper, aka Dan Cooper, aka the Skyjacker, is the only successful skyjacker to avoid capture.

2) Apparently, back then it only cost twenty dollars for a plane ticket, and you didn't even need ID or a passport to get on a plane, so no one knows what his real name was.

3) He hijacked a plane on November 24, 1971. He said he had a bomb and showed the flight attendant the wires and sticks hidden in his briefcase. They don't even know if it was real!

4) The bomb was convincing enough that the flight landed and he got people on the ground to bring $200,000 and four parachutes to the Seattle airport. They unloaded all the other passengers and gave him the money and the parachutes. Then the plane took off AGAIN, and flew south.

5) Using one parachute to hold the money and wearing another one, he jumped out of the hijacked plane with $200,000 in cash — somewhere between Seattle and Reno. He left behind two parachutes and only one other thing, his clip-on tie.

6) Neither he nor his body was ever found, so he might be ALIVE!!

7) Some people on the internet think that he could be living in Vancouver!

Armed with this knowledge of the case, I have opened a new case file, as I will devote my free time to finding the real D.B. Cooper, who could still be alive and well and living right next door.

Consider this file . . . OPEN.

END MISSIVE

This was the first time I had a case file that could be close to my house. A skyjacker, right here in Vancouver? This guy could be living one block away, and no one would ever know! Well, no one, until now. I was going to find D.B. Cooper. Maybe he could be a villain for the American Marmot comic too. Like, maybe he meets the American Marmot, who is also on the plane, and the American Marmot jumps out of the plane after him and they have an in-air parachute battle. It could be the first issue of the comic. Ali and I could probably get a big publishing contract and both get into the FBI if we solved it. I could have both of my dream jobs!

The problem was, I didn't really know where to start. I did some calculations in my head. The internet said that D.B. Cooper was maybe around thirty in 1971. That means I was looking for an old guy, someone around eighty years old. And there were plenty of old guys in our neighbourhood.

I decided that before doing anything, I should observe my surroundings. There was no need to complicate the case if D.B. Cooper was, in fact, living around the corner.

I had to wait though, because Mom kept me busy getting school stuff together on Monday, and then school started on Tuesday.

It turned out that Tristan and Ali were both in the other grade seven class, so I couldn't see Ali until recess. We met at our usual spot under the overhang. I got there first, and my heart sank a little when I saw that Tristan was walking over with him.

"Tristan was thinking we could play soccer!" Ali said as soon as I was within hearing distance.

"No thanks," I said.

"Hey, Coop! Come and play! It'll be awesome!" Tristan smiled broadly at me.

"CoopER," I said, stressing the last syllable. "And no thanks. Ali and I normally shoot hoops or play something else."

"Oh. Well. A bunch of our class talked about soccer." Tristan pointed at the field where the soccer game had already started.

"You can go," I said. "I don't want to." I turned to Ali. "I've got something cool to tell you about."

Ali looked over at the game. "I'm going to play. Is that okay? I . . . yeah . . . let's play soccer. Can you tell me later?"

But before I could answer, Ali and Tristan had run off to the field.

Ali totally ditched me on the first day of school! I made a decision to never tell him about the Cooper File. When he asked me at lunch I pretended to forget what I was talking about. Which sucked, because then I had to sit and listen to Tristan and Ali tell inside jokes from soccer camp. None of them were actually funny to me, so I tried to change the subject a few times to *The X-Files* or comics. It didn't really work. On the bus home after school, every story Ali told included Tristan too. By the time I got home, I wasn't sure who I was more annoyed by: Ali or Tristan.

It bothered me so much that I couldn't sit still. I was pacing around the house until I couldn't take it anymore. I didn't need Ali. I was going to solve my D.B. Cooper mystery alone. Dad was working on the neighbour's van and Mom wasn't home from work yet, so I knew I had time before dinner.

"Dad!" I called across the driveway to the legs sticking out from under the van. "I'm taking Dana Scully for a walk!"

Scully heard me and came bounding to the door, her tail wagging so hard it was like her butt was going to fall off.

"Be careful! Keep your eyes up! And no dark alleys!" Dad called out.

"No dark alleys," I promised. I put on Scully's leash, and we were off.

My first turn was down the alley. For one thing, it wasn't even dark yet. And I don't think that there are actually kidnappers biding their time, waiting for kids and their pets to walk down the alley they're hiding in. Plus, in our community the houses are much closer to the alley than they are to the actual street. This way I had a clearer view into people's kitchens. And since it was cloudy, people had their lights on, making it very easy to spy on them through the windows (a trick I learned from a spy book Ali had given me for my birthday last year). Despite being pulled forward by Scully, I made sure to slow down and observe each house. I pulled out my notebook and awkwardly shuffled the leash around my elbow so that I could write stuff down at each stop.

Scully and I made our way down the alley, looking through windows and then sprinting to the next house before stopping again. We did three full alleys before dinner. At that point, Scully and I turned up the brightly lit street and headed home.

When I got home, I went through the information I had and noted the addresses that I thought had some possibility:

450 Sherbrooke Street:
Old woman washing dishes. Where is her husband??

454 Sherbrooke Street:
Dead flowers on the windowsill. Thoughtful but forgetful old man??

462 Sherbrooke Street:
Young couple with a baby. Possible grandfather in the background?

463 Inverness Street:
Old man watching TV with old woman. Definitely possible!!

465 Inverness Street:
Lights are out. Not home, or in hiding? Follow up!

460 Culloden Street:
Lights are out. Follow up!

462 Culloden Street:
Lights are out. Conspiracy with neighbours? Follow up!

464 Culloden Street:
Old people standing around. A wake for the original D.B. Cooper?
Mafia meeting?? Could be any one of these people!!

468 Culloden Street:
Back of bald man's head watching TV. Definitely was a detective
show. Learning new skyjacking techniques?? Follow up!!

470 Culloden Street:
Old man eating dinner alone. Why does he eat so late? On the lam
from the police all day?? Follow up!

It felt like I had a lot to work with already. Obviously, more observation was necessary, but I had gotten a good start.

CHAPTER 4

Thursday at school, Tristan was gone over lunch for a dentist appointment. That meant I had Ali all to myself.

"So, what do you know about skyjackers?" I asked.

"Nothing," he said. "I don't even know what you're talking about."

"Like a guy who hijacks a plane," I explained.

Ali shrugged. "Know what I do know about? Fry-jackers. Like my dad, who always steals my fries if we go out."

I laughed. "Or maybe there's a pie-jacker. Someone who holds up bakeries in order to get free pies. He's like, 'Give me the banana cream and no one gets hurt . . .'"

"Or a tie-jacker. He's a businessman who steals other guys' ties when they're busy, like in the bathroom he pulls the ties off them."

We both laughed, then sat there trying to come up with more rhymes but couldn't. Even though I

25

had sworn I wouldn't tell Ali about D.B. Cooper, I couldn't keep it in anymore.

"There was this skyjacker I learned about who never got caught. Back in the seventies."

"No way," Ali said. "How do you hijack a plane and not get caught? You're making it up."

"You jump out of it," I said. Then I told him what I knew about D.B. Cooper.

"He didn't make it," Ali said matter-of-factly. "No way he survived."

"He could have," I countered. "No one ever found his body either. If he had died, don't you think they would have found his body?"

"Eaten by wolves and vultures," Ali said.

"I don't think so. A guy smart enough to plan a hijacking isn't going to die when he lands. This is, like, the biggest unsolved FBI case ever."

"I don't know. I think the dude is super dead. Splat! And it kind of serves him right for being a criminal. Oh, did Tristan talk to you? His birthday party is on Saturday and my sister said she can drive us."

"He never told me that he invited me," I said. It came out sounding sulkier than I wanted it to.

"Well, you're definitely invited. We can go together," Ali said like it was a done deal.

I didn't want to go to Tristan's birthday, but I didn't have a good reason for not going, and I figured that showing up with Ali would prove that we were best friends, so I asked my mom if I could go.

She said yes, but then grumbled about how I left it to the last minute to get him a present.

It was raining hard on Saturday.

"Mom! I don't have any rain pants!" I yelled down the hall when I was getting ready. Tristan never mentioned anything about the party to me, so I didn't know if we were going to have to play soccer or something dumb like that. I didn't put it past him, and I wanted to be ready to go outside.

"Use mine. They're in the back closet!"

"I can't wear your pants! They're for girls!" I responded.

Mom appeared at the top of the stairs.

"They're black rain pants. They aren't for girls or boys. They're unisex, Cooper," she said. "Roll up the bottoms and you'll be fine."

"Can't we just go buy me some?" I asked.

"You have literally never asked to wear rain pants before in your life. We're not buying you your own pair. Use mine." Mom walked away, then came back a moment later holding her rain pants. "Don't get them wet," she said, as she handed them to me.

"What . . . Mom! How am I . . . ?"

"Kidding, Cooper. I'm kidding."

I put on the dumb lady rain pants. "If I die today, tell everyone it wasn't my idea to die wearing ladies' clothes," I called as I left.

"Then don't die today," Mom called back. "Be careful walking to Ali's. Don't dawdle. And come straight home after the party. You have the present?"

"Yeah. Right here," I said, showing her the plastic bag with the wrapped-up puzzle. I didn't really know Tristan, so we went to the games place by our house and bought him a jigsaw puzzle, which seems weird, but I liked puzzles, so maybe Tristan did too.

I was soaked when I got to Ali's house, both outside and inside the rain pants. I had no idea rain gear was so hot! Ali was sitting by the door waiting for me, reading a comic.

"You can't wear that," he said. "You look super dumb. What did you bring for a present?"

I kicked off my boots and peeled off the rain pants. "A puzzle," I said. "Can I leave these here?"

Ali pointed to the hooks beside the door. "Like a jigsaw puzzle? You can't bring a jigsaw puzzle. That's lame. Sign your name to my gift. It's a video game. Tristan talked about it at soccer so I know he wants it."

"Oh. Okay." I signed his card. I was kind of glad that Ali had suggested it. It would show Tristan that Ali and I were best friends. I put the puzzle on the hook, over Mom's rain pants.

"'Kay. Surya! Let's go!" Ali called to his sister, who was driving us to the party.

When we got there Tristan flashed me a huge smile. "Coop! I didn't know you were coming! That's awesome!" He seemed a bit confused.

"Ali said I was invited," I said, unsure of what to do. "I mean, I can go . . ."

"No way, man. It's cool. I mean, we were supposed

to only be ten, but I guess we're eleven now. That's cool. It'll just be weird for pizza," he said.

I shrugged. "I'm not starving," I said. "Don't worry about me." I was feeling like coming to the party was a bad idea.

Ali had already abandoned me to talk to Stephanie about *Minecraft*, so I was on my own, watching kids trade off *Mario Kart* turns. I sat quietly on the couch, behind everyone sitting on the floor. They were laughing and teasing each other and shoving chips in their mouths. I ate a few pretzels out of the bowl beside the couch, but they were super stale. I didn't really know what to do to feel like part of the party, so I tried to tell them about the D.B. Cooper case.

"Hey, did you guys know that in the seventies a guy jumped out of a plane with a ton of money and was never found?"

Ali turned around, and so did Tristan.

"Seriously?" Tristan said.

"It's cool. He, like, hijacked a plane and was never found after he jumped out with the ransom money," I said. I told them more of the story of D.B. Cooper.

Tristan laughed. "Oh man. We should find him. I bet the reward money is massive."

I felt the threat of competition; it came up fast and intense. "I am going to find him. I already started looking for him this week. I know where he could be hiding," I boasted.

"Right. You're going to find him? I'll give you a thousand bucks if you do," Tristan said.

I sat up straight and tried to look confident. "Oh yeah? Seriously?"

Tristan raised his eyebrows at me. His look had a competitive edge. He grinned.

"Wanna make a bet? If you find this guy, I'll give you a hundred bucks. If you don't find him, you owe me that money."

"Deal," I said. I could seriously use a hundred bucks. Plus, I was smarter than Tristan. He never said how long I had to find him.

"Guys," Ali said. "Guys, this is dumb. Hey, is the pizza ready?" He tried to change the subject.

"Wait! You should set a time limit," said Stephanie, who was watching the whole exchange. In fact, I noticed that everyone had stopped even playing video games. "AND shake on it."

Stephanie was known in our class for being the most fair, which I normally liked, but I wasn't happy that she pointed out my loophole.

"Oh yeah. Okay. One week," Tristan said.

"No way. That's not long enough, and you know it!" I said.

"Fine. One month. And you need to prove it. Like, real proof. Deal?"

I knew Tristan's dad was super rich. Ali told me that Tristan always had a new phone or he had the best cleats. I, on the other hand, definitely did not have a hundred dollars. Mom and Dad were constantly talking about money these days, and I wasn't even allowed to get good pencil crayons.

"You make it two months and you've got a deal," I said. "Let's shake on it."

**

"Why did you make that bet?" Ali pounced on me as soon as we got in the car to go home. "You know Tristan will follow through, right? Are you crazy?"

"I don't know why. He was annoying me," I said. "But can you imagine how good it would be if I won? That would be amazing."

Ali shook his head. "You can't win. You aren't going to solve the biggest unsolved mystery in fifty years, and especially not in one month."

"I have two months," I said.

Ali clearly didn't believe it, but I did. I could win this bet. Why not? I'd already started the research. Were FBI agents even allowed to look in Canada? They might have had to give up just because of the border.

"Maybe we can look around this week," I said. "We could walk around and spy on people."

"No way. I'm not getting involved. You're on your own with this one. I'm a neutral party."

"Fine. Watch me. I'll solve this mystery and Tristan will give me a ton of money." I sounded more confident than I felt. I didn't want to think about the fact that I didn't have the money. I had to focus on the positive and start solving my case.

CHAPTER 5

I spent Saturday night on the computer, trying to find out more about D.B. Cooper and looking at maps of Vancouver. If I was going to win this bet, I needed to be prepared. I couldn't wait to walk up to Tristan and demand my money, and when he asked why, I could point to this unmarked car that would be parked across the street from my house.

In the front seat, there would be two mysterious guys wearing dark shades and black suits, and in the back, an old guy in handcuffs. They would nod at me knowingly, and the old guy would hold up his handcuffed arms and shake them at me in anger.

"That's why," I would say. It was going to be perfect. But I needed time and more information. Luckily, Mom didn't want the computer and Dad was watching hockey at the neighbour's, so I had time to find out so much stuff.

I got distracted, though, listening to Mom on the phone with her friend Marilyn. I wasn't going to listen, but I heard her say my name so I opened the door to the computer room a bit. ". . . school supplies are out of control these days. How can schools ask us to spend that much right off the bat? . . . Yeah, well, there's that too . . . With Dad being in the new ward, it's so much more expensive. All the extra care, and they can basically charge what they want knowing we have no other option."

Why did Mom have to pay for Grandpa? I thought about all the money he had given me. I assumed he was rich.

". . . Marco? No help at all. It's so frustrating. I want to just throttle him sometimes . . ."

This wasn't good. I opened the door a bit more and wheeled my chair right next to the door jamb. "I wish. I suggested therapy, and he was totally against it. We can't afford it anyway . . . I don't know . . . We never should have gone on vacation this summer. It was double what I had budgeted, and more stressful than relaxing spending all that time together, that's for sure. I'm going to try and pick up some shifts at Kingsgate Dental if I can, and I changed our phone plans to the most basic option, but it's not helping. But enough of this. I feel like all I do is complain these days. How was Scotland? Your cousin is doing better?"

I sat quietly, but Mom's conversation moved on to less interesting topics. I closed the door and went back to the computer. I was distracted, though. I didn't know what would happen if we had no money. I realized that winning this bet was more important than just showing up Tristan. I needed it for my family's survival.

The next day Mom refused to let me bring my tablet to Golden Sunsets, so I needed to find a way to make a day with Grandpa more interesting.

"Can I bring Dana Scully?" I asked Mom, as we were getting ready.

"I don't think so. She's probably not allowed," she replied.

"But she's really cute. And Grandpa likes dogs. And they have dogs there all the time. There are dogs who live there full-time. Therapy dogs or whatever," I countered.

"But they know those dogs." Mom clearly didn't want to bring Dana Scully, but I was persistent.

"She'll be good, won't you, Scully?" Scully kissed my face and wagged her tail. "Look how excited she is to go. Otherwise, she's just going to be underfoot in the garage," I said, loud enough that my dad could hear me.

"Take the dog! Please!" I heard him chime in.

"Fine. But if they don't let her come in, you're the one who has to sit outside with her."

I smiled. "Of course! C'mon, Scully! We're going on a car ride!" Scully wagged her tail and followed me to the car.

Golden Sunsets looked even more depressing in the rain, since they turned on more lights inside. The fluorescent bulbs in the hallways gave everyone even more of a deathly glow than normal. I held

Scully tight in my arms as she squirmed to get down. Mom tapped in the code at Grandpa's ward and signed us in at the front desk.

"We're here to see Don Cooke," she said. "And we brought our dog. Is that okay?"

The nurse-receptionist wasn't paying any attention. "Oh, fine. Just don't let him down."

"She's a she. Her name is Dana Scully," I pointed Dana toward the woman.

"Mmmhmm," she said, already turned back to her computer.

Mom was in the room scanning for Grandpa. She spotted him over by a window, at one of the card tables.

"Hi, Dad! It's your daughter Dawn," she said loudly. "I've brought your grandson, Cooper, with me to visit. And he brought you a surprise!"

"Looking good, little lady! Oh, it's nice to see you!" Grandpa smiled fondly at Mom.

"And you. Look at how he's grown! God, I haven't seen you in a dog's age!" He smiled at me, and I was reminded of what it was like to see Grandpa before he was sick, when he was fun and always knew who I was and greeted me like I was the only person he wanted to see. He pulled out his wallet and, with a flourish, handed me an American one-dollar bill. "In case of emergencies," he said, with a wink.

I grabbed it with one hand, still holding on to a squirming Dana Scully. "Thanks so much,

Grandpa. I brought my dog to meet you." I held Dana Scully in his direction.

He laughed and held out his arms to hold her. "And who is this little furry face? Look at that face! He looks like a Muppet!" I handed Dana over to Grandpa. She wriggled about in his lap and turned to lick his face. Grandpa laughed. "Outta my face, you mutt! Oh, you're a cute little thing! Ahh, stop it!"

Mom laughed too. "Her name is Dana Scully, Dad. We got her from a shelter this summer. Cooper named her after a TV character."

"Well, Dana Scully, you sure are a ball of fluff!" Grandpa was smiling broadly, alternating between me and Dana. I looked at Mom, and she nodded at me. Bringing Dana Scully was a hit!

"Dana Scully is a TV detective, Grandpa," I explained. "She's from my favourite TV show, *The X-Files*. She solves unsolvable mysteries."

"Oh yeah? Sounds like a good program." Grandpa was still burying his face in Scully's fur and baby-talking to her absentmindedly.

"Yeah. Dana Scully works with this guy Fox Mulder and they solve all kinds of cases that no one else can solve, like about aliens and ghosts and stuff. Mom thinks it's too scary for me to watch so I barely get to see any of the episodes, but it's from the nineties, and nothing old is scary anymore." I looked at Mom pointedly. She rolled her eyes at me. "Anyway," I continued, "Mulder and Scully could probably even solve the case of D.B. Cooper."

At that, Grandpa looked up at me. "What did you say?"

I heard Mom sigh next to me. There was a distinct shift in the mood around the table for everyone except Scully, who was still burrowing into Grandpa's elbow.

"I said that Mulder and Scully could solve the mystery of D.B. Cooper. You talked about him last week when we were here."

"No, I didn't," Grandpa said.

"Yes, you did. You said that the internet didn't know who D.B. Cooper was. So I looked him up. Nobody knows who he was, other than a skyjacker. He got a ton of money and then jumped out of a plane between Seattle and Reno back in the seventies. It said that he could be living in Vancouver. I've been looking for him in our neighbourhood. But if *The X-Files* was real, Mulder and Scully would be able to find him."

"Cooper, D.B. Cooper doesn't live here. Those are a bunch of conspiracy theorists making stuff up. Plus, there's a Vancouver in Washington too. And it's much closer to Seattle. They probably mean Vancouver, Washington," Mom said.

Grandpa looked agitated. "Why are we talking about D.B. Cooper?" he said. "I don't want to talk about D.B. Cooper."

"But last week you brought him up!" I persisted.

"No, I didn't."

"Yes, you did. I looked him up. He successfully

skyjacked a plane, maybe even without having a real bomb. And no one knows who he is!" I said.

"No!" Grandpa stood up, sending Dana Scully to the floor. Scully took the opportunity to run off to the other side of the common room.

"Cooper! Get the dog!"

"Dana! Dana!" I called to her, but she decided that this was the moment to play. She barked at me and raced around the chairs. The old people were startled, and one of the women started to yell.

"Cooper!" Mom called to me again.

"I'm trying!" I lunged at Dana Scully as she ran past me to do another loop around the room.

"Cooper! Get the dog!"

"Ma'am, you need to get your dog." The nurse-receptionist had come over from behind her desk and was standing next to my mother. The old woman was still yelling, and another nurse came rushing into the room, shooting me a look of pure hate.

"DANA! DANA SCULLY!" I tried to back her into a corner, but Scully wagged her tail and barked before shooting off toward the yelling woman. The woman started yelling louder and was soon joined by another woman, who started crying. One of the men started cheering me on, pumping his arms and yelling, "Go, boy!" He laughed at the scene, but I was in a panic. Scully wouldn't stop, running as though she had never run before.

"Control your dog!" the mean nurse yelled.

"I'm trying!" I snapped.

And precisely at the moment that Scully was rounding the corner by the reception desk, the door buzzed and unlocked. Scully ducked out the door as it slowly opened on its own.

"Cooper!" My mom was freaking out.

"Scully!" I was freaking out.

Grandpa, on the other hand, took this moment to assert his earlier denial. "I don't know anything about D.B. Cooper!" he called out.

I was trapped as the door opened slowly on its own. On the other side was a man using a walker, flanked by two men, both of whom were turned around, watching my dog scamper down the long hallway.

"Excuse me!" I dodged past the men and took off at a full run after Scully.

It was quieter in the hallway, with only a few people in wheelchairs parked around the windows. I finally spotted Scully sitting at the feet of an Asian lady perched on a bench near the front door. Scully had her paws up on the lady's knees and was happily getting her head scratched.

I stopped in front of the lady, who looked up and smiled at me. She was short, with a long white braid over her shoulder. The lady was dressed like she was going to work at an office, wearing a light pink blouse and a grey skirt, but with a pair of bright green loafers that didn't match anything else she had on. She looked younger than most of the other residents at Golden Sunsets.

"Is this your little guy?" she asked. "He's adorable!"

"It's a she," I panted. "Her name is Dana Scully."

The woman perked up. "Like *The X-Files*? Oh, how wonderful! I just loved that show!" Her eyes twinkled and almost disappeared into the wrinkles of her round cheeks when she smiled.

I sat down next to her and grabbed Scully, pulling her into my lap to make sure she wouldn't run off again.

"I know. It's so great. I wish I could watch it all but my parents won't let me watch it at home. I watch them at my best friend's house," I explained.

"Oh, I understand that. It can be quite a shocker! No doubt about that. No nine-year-old should be watching that show."

I frowned. "I'm twelve. And it's not that scary. It's just cool. The mysteries are cool."

"I do love the mysteries! I love unexplained phenomena. I have some books about it. I should bring them for you! Would you like to see them? They are fascinating. Did you know that I have a bit of ESP?" She smiled at me.

"Really?" I asked.

"Yes, yes. At least, I used to. I have a touch of the Alzheimer's now, so my memory isn't what it used to be."

I looked at her skeptically. She seemed way more with it than the rest of the people in Grandpa's ward. Although, I didn't know what she was doing outside the locked door. I looked back down the hall to see if anyone was looking for her.

The woman noticed. "Oh, I don't live here. My husband drops me off for the day so that he can take a little break. Living with me is most certainly not the easiest thing to do!" she said with a chuckle. "But it sure was a delight to meet you and Dana Scully today. I've never met a television star before!" She ruffled Scully's fur.

At that moment, a man approached us.

"Ah, my darling husband! He came back this time!" she laughed and stood up, so I did too. I was at least a head taller than her when we were standing.

He smiled. "I always do."

"I don't know why. I'm a bear to live with!" They both chuckled at what was clearly an inside joke.

"Darling husband, this is the famous Dana Scully, and . . . oh dear. Did you tell me your name? Did I forget it already?" The woman looked instantly distressed.

"No. I never told you," I assured her. "I'm Cooper."

"I am Yireh Kim, and this is my husband, Juno Kim." The man tipped his hat to me, and Mrs. Kim did a little bow. "At least, I think that's our names!" She laughed again, and so did he.

It was weird. No one in my family ever laughed at the things that Grandpa forgot. I couldn't believe Mrs. Kim thought it was funny.

"Nice to meet you. I should, um, I should probably get back to my grandpa," I said.

"Maybe I'll see you again. I'll bring you those books." She turned to Mr. Kim. "Remember that we are supposed to bring the mystery books for . . ." She paused. "Um . . ."

"Cooper," I supplied. "I'm here every Sunday too."

"Well, then I will see you next Sunday." Mrs. Kim stepped in and gave me a hug that was warm and strong. I still had Scully in my arms, so I stood there while she hugged me and Scully together.

"Okay . . . um. Bye," I said, pulling away.

Mr. Kim smiled and nodded at me as they turned to leave. I watched as Mrs. Kim hooked her arm on Mr. Kim's and they headed to the exit. I wished that my parents held hands. They never did stuff like that. I kissed Dana Scully's head as I buzzed myself into Grandpa's ward and went to find Mom.

CHAPTER 6

Mom was, like usual, in a foul mood on the way home. She lectured me on being more responsible; she complained about the traffic; she talked about Dad being useless in assisting with Grandpa. She complained about every topic she could. I sat silently while she went on and on, wishing that I could have my old mom back. She was getting worse, and I could understand why my dad stayed late at the garage or worked on his car when he was home. I wanted to do that too. It wasn't just Dad and me that annoyed her, it seemed to be everything.

I avoided her angry vacuuming and kitchen cleaning and spent most of the evening learning things about D.B. Cooper.

It was a real blow to learn that Mom was right — there is another Vancouver that is only a five-hour drive from regular Vancouver, and it's way closer to the spot where D.B. Cooper was supposed to have landed. I don't know why people on the internet didn't specify which Vancouver they meant.

This threw a wrench into my finding D.B. Cooper. I asked Dad if we could go to Vancouver, Washington, the next weekend, but he looked at me like I was crazy and said no. I was starting to worry about the bet. Tristan's mom and dad were both lawyers, so they made a hundred dollars in, like, five minutes. And after hearing Mom talking about money and debt yesterday, I could never ask her to borrow that much. I had to win.

I thought about contacting one of the pilots or the flight attendant to find out more, but my phone privileges have been really limited since earlier this year when I called Scotland and chatted with a Loch Ness monster expert for an hour. To be fair, it was very helpful in learning more about what I should be looking for in my search for Ogopogo, but Dad didn't see the value in it.

I did get a real feel for what D.B. Cooper looked like in my internet searches. In all the sketches, he looked like a movie star, like one of those guys who would always be wearing a cowboy hat and boots. Maybe he was that guy. I also found out that he might have stolen the name Dan Cooper from some popular Belgian comic book, and that Dan Cooper in the comic was a Royal Canadian Air Force test pilot. This guy must be super cool if he was a comic book fan.

Other passengers reported that he was tall, and he had perfectly combed hair (they didn't say that, but I could tell from the drawings). If he wasn't a cowboy, I bet he was a soldier. I read about how the Vietnam War was on at the time, and some men were trying to not have to fight. They were called draft dodgers, and some of them did crazy things to get out of going to fight. But I don't think he was one of those. After all, he had to have parachute experience to be able to open a plane door and jump out and survive. He even had an altimeter on him to make sure that the pilot didn't fly too high for him to be able to survive a jump. That's planning. How does a guy know that without ever having jumped out of a plane before? Some sites said that he must have been in the parachute corps in the army, and I think I'm with them.

The more I read about this D.B. Cooper guy, the crazier he seemed. How did he just saunter onto a plane, super chill, have a drink, then tell the flight attendant to get them to land the plane because he had a bomb? That happened? In real life? Who WAS this guy?

What I really needed was another agent on the case. Dana Scully, although named for a very excellent detective, was pretty useless when it came to solving anything. I had thought that having a dog would be really good for sniffing out crime and unexplained phenomena, but Scully had a really hard time staying properly focused when she got excited. I missed Ali. I couldn't believe he didn't want to help me.

On Monday Tristan, Ali and I sat together at

lunch. I was stewing sitting there, especially since Tristan didn't even bring up our bet. It was like he assumed that I was going to lose and he wasn't going to say anything, just quietly be smug about it.

He was talking about this movie he had watched the night before when I interrupted him.

"I made inroads on my case already," I said.

He looked confused at the change of subject. "Oh. Cool?"

"Yeah. I know what city he's in. It's either Vancouver, B.C., or Vancouver, Washington."

Tristan laughed. "There's no such place!"

"There is too. Look it up." I felt way smarter than him just by knowing that. I looked over at Ali and grinned knowingly, like we were both on the same side of an inside joke. He looked confused too, and a little annoyed with me.

"Um. I'm going to go outside. You guys should come." Tristan got up, clearly uncomfortable that I was so much smarter than him.

"Gonna finish my sandwich, then we'll be there," Ali responded. Tristan nodded and left.

Ali looked at me weirdly. "What's up with you, dude?"

"I can win this thing, Ali. Just you watch. Or you could help me."

Ali just changed the subject. "Hey, wanna go to the library sale after school? They are selling off a bunch of books and comics and stuff. My mom got an invitation to the pre-sale because she's a volunteer.

She said there were a bunch of comics, and they're only, like, a quarter each. It could be worth it."

"Is Tristan coming?" I asked.

"Nah. Just us." Ali sounded almost sad about it, but I pretended not to notice that part.

"Sounds good," I said. "Let me call my mom and tell her. I'll go to the office now."

"I'm gonna go find Tristan. Come out when you're done."

We headed to the library after school and met Ali's mom there.

"Twenty minutes, okay, boys? We have to leave by four-thirty," she said. We nodded and headed straight to the comic section.

"Hey, Cooper! Look at this! Captain Canuck! He's like a lamer version of Captain America!" Ali said, holding up a battered comic.

"Why is he lame? He's Canadian. That automatically makes him cooler," I said.

Ali handed me the comic. "Except look at this." The cover had a beaver, a moose and a Mountie, all being saved from going over Niagara Falls by Captain Canuck. We laughed.

"We should change the American Marmot. Make him Canadian. There are no good Canadian superheroes," Ali said.

"Wolverine is Canadian," I argued.

"Except Wolverine."

"So instead of the American Marmot, we make him, what?" I asked.

"The Canada Goose!" Ali said.

"With powers of projectile poo!" I added.

"A turd tornado!" Ali said.

We laughed hysterically until a volunteer asked us to be quieter. I couldn't, though, because every time I looked at Ali, we started laughing again. I finally moved away into the non-fiction section. I found a couple of old books from a series on mysteries of the unknown. There was one on alien abductions and another on mystic places. They looked like the books that Mrs. Kim had talked about.

"Five minutes, kids," Mrs. Singh called.

Ali had a stack of comics in his arms. "Look at this! All this is only three bucks!"

"Good deal," I said. "I'm going to get these two. Do you think your mom can lend me two dollars?"

"Totally!" Ali said, but he was so wrapped up in flipping through his comic finds that I don't think he knew what he was agreeing to.

Mrs. Singh paid for my books and drove me home. When I got there, Mom and Dad were in the middle of an argument. They stopped as I came in the door.

"Cooper! Come set the table, please," Dad called. "I'm going to take the chicken off the barbecue."

The Canada Goose and his trusty sidekick, Barbecue Chicken, I said to myself, wishing I was eating dinner at Ali's house.

CHAPTER 7

A couple of nights later I could hear Mom and Dad arguing after I went to bed. Mom complained about what they were watching on TV, and they got going from there. When it got too hard to make out what they were saying from inside my room, I got up to stand at the top of the stairs.

I don't know why I did it; I hated listening to them fight. It always started about dumb stuff that would be easily solved if one of them just gave in. That's what I did with Ali when he wanted to argue. But they didn't — they just kept finding more stuff to argue about.

Tonight they were fighting about the cost of Grandpa's care home, and how my Aunt Jane wasn't pitching in. And then they moved on to how my dad wasn't being supportive, but that my mom was shutting him out, and on and on.

What if they got divorced? I didn't know a lot of kids with divorced parents. There were a couple in my class, but other than that, I only knew married people. I sat on the stairs with Dana Scully in my lap. Would I live with Mom or Dad? Mom was being weird and grumpy these days, but Dad was always at work. I leaned my head against the wall. I wished there was something I could do to make them stop fighting and make them happy again.

I heard the door to the garage open and close, so I hurried to my bed and jumped under the covers.

"Cooper? Are you still up?" Mom called, but I knew better than to answer. She came into my room. "I know you're still awake. I'm going out for a bit. Dad's in the garage if you need anything." She kissed my forehead. "Love you. And go to sleep."

The next day, Mom had clearly gone shopping on her lunch break, because there was a brand-new floral notebook on the table after school. I flipped through it, but it was empty.

"I hope this isn't for me," I said. "I prefer pink roses."

She laughed, then took it out of my hands and stroked the cover. "Marilyn suggested I write down Grandpa's stories, maybe make a family scrapbook for him." She sounded kind of excited about it. I didn't want to mention the scrap of paper Grandpa kept with him to remind him who his family was.

"Good idea, Mom," I said. She smiled a real smile, not like the strained smiles that normally came whenever we talked about Grandpa. "Don't forget it on Sunday." I looked around. "What did you buy me?"

She swatted at me lightly with the notebook. "Nothing, smart aleck. Has Dana Scully gone out yet?"

***

On Sunday, after the car was parked but before we got out, Mom turned to me. "No D.B. Cooper stuff today. No mysteries. Let's keep it light. Got it?" she said.

"Yeah, yeah," I replied. "Do you have your notebook?"

"I'm serious, Cooper. Let's try and get through today without any major breakdowns," she said.

"Mom. I got it. I promise not to talk about anything. We're only learning stories about Grandpa."

Every week was a new week with Grandpa. When we came in, the nurse-receptionist (who gave me a very cold look and asked if I had a dog with me) informed Mom that Grandpa was refusing to leave his room. He was stating that there was someone in the main room who had gas so bad that, and she quoted him, "It rivalled the stench of a thousand rotting whale carcasses." (To be fair, he was right. We had to walk through the main room and I almost threw up it stank so bad.)

So we crowded into his little bedroom. Mom was sitting on the bed, Grandpa was in his ratty teal armchair watching TV, and I was standing, moving aimlessly around the small area between them both. I couldn't tell if he knew who we were, but he definitely did not go for his wallet this time.

I thought about asking, but Mom could tell where I was headed and started talking first.

"Hi, Dad. Cooper and I thought it would be fun to make a scrapbook of our family. Doesn't that sound fun? I'm hoping you can help us out."

Grandpa looked at her and shrugged. "No thanks." He turned up the TV.

We sat there. Mom grasped her notebook. She flipped it open and closed, looking at the blank pages. It made me feel bad for her, so I tried to get the conversation started.

"Who are the photos of?" I asked Mom. I pointed at the photos lined up on Grandpa's windowsill.

"What?" Grandpa turned and looked at me blankly. I picked up the black-and-white photo and held it toward him.

"Who is this?" I said.

"Dunno," he said. He shot me a look, like my talking was getting in the way of his PBS special.

"Those are my grandparents," Mom said in almost a whisper, as if finding that out would set Grandpa off.

"They were American?" I asked, pointing to the American flag in the background.

"And proud as punch of it!" she said.

I looked at Mom quizzically. "You're American?" I asked her.

"No. I was born here. But Grandpa was born in the States, weren't you, Dad?" I hated the way Mom always spoke louder and slower to him. He was silent, so Mom continued. "Born and raised in Chicago, Illinois."

"That's the home of the World's Fair," Grandpa said to the TV. "The Windy City."

That explained why he always had American money. I just thought he liked it.

"When did you come to Canada?" I asked.

"When did you come to Canada, Dad?" Mom had her pen at the ready to record this detail. "Do you remember?"

"A long time ago," he responded.

She spoke quietly to me. "He met Grandma in the States earlier and moved to Canada in 1972. Then they had me and your Auntie Jane. See? Here's a photo of all four of us!" Mom pulled out the photo album from her youth that sat on the shelf.

"Look, Dad. Here's photos of me and my sister, Jane, when we were born. How did you feel when we were born?" she asked, prodding for anything to put in her notebook.

He glanced briefly at the photos, then his attention went back to the TV. "Old, probably."

I laughed. It was kind of mean, but it was funny that he was making Mom's scrapbook activity harder.

"Dad." Mom was almost whining. She sounded like a teenager. "Can you help me out here? I'm making this for you."

"Don't bother," he said.

Silence descended on the room again. I picked

up the photo closest to me. It was a black-and-white photo of Grandpa and Grandma when they were younger. Grandpa had a full head of hair, perfectly coifed in that weird greasy way you see in old photos. He was tall and thin and stared, unsmiling, at the camera. He looked familiar, but not in the way I thought, not like a young version of the guy in front of me. He looked like one of those old-time movie stars, those guys who you can't name but you see their pictures a lot.

Mom flipped through the photo album a little longer, but she wasn't trying to write anything down anymore. Finally, she put it back and stood up.

"Well, Dad, Cooper has got lots of homework tonight, so we're going to have to cut our visit short," Mom announced.

Grandpa kind of grunted as a response. I made a mental note to try that at home. Mom kissed the top of his head, and we left.

I noticed Mrs. Kim sitting on the bench by the door on our way out.

"Hi, Mrs. Kim!" I stopped in front of her.

"Hello, dear," she said, smiling. "Have we met? Oh, wait. We must have. Otherwise how would you know my name?" She chuckled.

"Yeah. I met you last week. I had my dog, Dana Scully, with me," I reminded her.

"Dana Scully. What a great detective! I'm sorry I don't remember that. I have a touch of the

Alzheimer's, you know. I'm waiting for my husband to pick me up," she said.

"I know. This is where we met last week. You were even going to bring me some books on mysteries," I said.

Mom looked at me funny. "Honey, we have to go. Dad's waiting for us at home," she said. Then, turning to Mrs. Kim, "We have to be going."

Mrs. Kim smiled widely. "Of course! Of course! I won't keep you here! It was nice to meet you, young man. Say hi to Dana Scully for me."

I nodded. "I sure will. And maybe if you remember, you could bring those books. I found some this week too. I'll show you. Or maybe next week I'll be allowed to bring my dog back!" By this point Mom was literally pulling me toward the door. "Bye!" I called.

When we got in the car, I turned to Mom. "What was that for? She's a nice lady who I met last week. I'm not seven. I can talk to strangers, you know."

"Cooper, I don't want you upsetting any of the patients there. You know how agitated Grandpa gets. It's not just him, it's everyone there. They don't want to be reminded that they can't remember things. Live in the present. We've talked about this. Poor Mrs. Kim's husband probably isn't even coming," Mom said.

"Yes, he is, Mom. I met him last week too. Not everyone is totally out of it, you know."

We drove home in silence. When we got there, I

went straight to the den and closed the door. It has a glass door, so you can still see in, but it was more of a symbolic "leave me alone" gesture.

I went to check out some of my bookmarked D.B. Cooper sites. If nothing else, mystery solving would get my mind off the afternoon. I started scanning the sites for new information. I was clicking through mindlessly, not paying attention to the numerous conspiracy theories and possible D.B. Coopers out there.

There was a scratch at the door. I spun the chair and wheeled myself over to it. I opened it a crack to let Dana Scully in. She immediately jumped up onto my lap, so I closed the door and shuffled my feet to pull the chair back to the computer. But something caught my eye; it wasn't the computer, but a photo in Mom's family gallery.

It was a black-and-white photo of Grandpa as a young man. I stared at it, getting close to the photo and pulling away, then I looked at the computer screen, where a composite drawing of D.B. Cooper was half-visible. I scrolled down to see the whole thing, then looked back at the photograph on the wall. Back and forth, back and forth.

The two pictures looked the same.

I mean, not exactly the same, but close. Same high forehead. Same thin nose and straight hairline. Same eyebrows that almost met in the middle. I have those eyebrows too. Grandpa even had the same kind of sunglasses. I remembered how he kept a pair in his car, and I used to put them on when we would go for drives.

Grandpa was American. He came to Canada in 1972, according to Mom, which was one year after D.B. Cooper jumped from the plane. He looked like D.B. Cooper. He freaked out when we talked about D.B. Cooper.

When looking at everything put together, all signs pointed to Yes. I nudged Dana Scully off my lap and lifted the photo off the wall. I put it up beside the computer.

"Dana Scully," I said, "I think my grandfather is a famous hijacker."

CHAPTER 8

I called Ali right after supper to tell him my theory of D.B. Grandpa.

"Yeah . . ." He made the word last forever. "But his name isn't D.B. Cooper."

"Of course it isn't. That was probably just the cover name he gave to get on the plane. Or maybe that WAS his real name, but after the skyjacking he changed it to Don. It's not that far off. Dan could equal Don. Cooke is practically Cooper. It's not that hard to forge stuff like that."

"I don't know, dude. It doesn't make sense. It's too easy."

"But even my name, Ali! My parents always said that my grandpa helped pick my name. Why would he choose Cooper if it didn't mean anything?"

"Still. Even if it's true, Tristan won't believe you."

"He'll have to. I'm going to prove it." I stopped to think. "Maybe my grandpa was going to tell me later in life, but then he got Alzheimer's. Or he was going to tell me on his deathbed, like in the movies.

Maybe he didn't trust my dad; maybe he thought Dad would rat him out. So then he was waiting for me to be old enough to be trustworthy."

"Yeah, okay. Sure. Hey, guess what? One of the comics I got at the library is gold!" Ali was trying to change the subject, but I wasn't ready to let it go.

"Ali, this could be huge! My grandpa is a known criminal to everyone in the world except himself!" I thought a bit longer. "Or what if . . . what if he is faking the Alzheimer's thing because the Feds were getting close to finding him? What if this whole thing is part of his escape plan?"

"No way. Dude. Your grandpa is not an airplane hijacker, he's not faking losing his memory, you're going to lose this bet to Tristan and you're definitely not going to get some big secret revealed to you when your grandpa's on his deathbed. Sorry, but you gotta hear it from someone. I already told you that this skyjacker is definitely super dead. Besides, I have news too. Real news. One of the comics I got is this super old Batman. Like soooooooper old — 1955 old. I think it's gotta be worth money. Lots of money."

Ali didn't believe me, so I decided not to believe him. "Yeah right. Any comic worth money isn't just old. It has to be unique in some way."

"Well, I think this one could be worth a bunch. Imagine if it's worth a million bucks? If I had a million bucks, I would give both you and Tristan a hundred bucks so that I didn't have to hear about this bet anymore."

"I gotta go," I said, tired of talking to him. "I still have math homework to do."

"Okay. I'm gonna bring the comic to school tomorrow. I'll show you how cool it is!"

I hung up kind of angry. Why didn't Ali take my side ever anymore? I was his best friend, but it sure seemed like he thought Tristan should win our bet. I wanted to hate Tristan, but I couldn't, not really. But I did hate him for trying to steal my friend. I didn't have anyone else but Ali. Everyone seemed to like Tristan. He could be best friends with literally anyone else.

I turned and spotted Dana Scully napping beside her food bowl. I relaxed a little. At least I had her. I bet Tristan didn't have a dog as cute as mine.

CASE: 0024 / FILE: 0002
LOCATION: Vancouver, British Columbia

In order to fully investigate the hypothesis that D.B. Cooper is, in fact, Don Cooke, grandfather to Agent Cooper Arcano, interviews with the alleged skyjacker's family are imperative. The first interview was conducted during the ritual watching of television on Monday evening, after ensuring that all members of the interview were calm and relatively happy.

AGENT COOPER: What was Grandpa like when you were younger?

AGENT DAWN COOKE-ARCANO (DAUGHTER OF D.B. COOPER): Sorry, sweetheart? I couldn't hear you.

Marco, the TV doesn't need to be that loud.

AGENT MARCO ARCANO (SON-IN-LAW OF D.B. COOPER): WHAT?? I can't hear you. The TV is too loud.

AGENT COOPER: What was Grandpa like when you were younger? What did he do?

AGENT DAWN: Oh, he was a . . . He was . . . What is going on? Why is there a hockey game on? Marco, no. I don't want to watch hockey.

AGENT COOPER: Mom!

AGENT DAWN: Sorry. Grandpa was an accountant. Or a comptroller or something. Something to do with numbers. He didn't want to work with people.

AGENT MARCO: Not a surprise. He was a jerk to me when we met.

AGENT DAWN: Ha! Of course he was. You came waltzing into his house to take away his eldest daughter.

AGENT MARCO: Seriously, Cooper. I thought he was going to shoot me. He grilled me for half an hour before we could leave. I was thinking, "Ohhhh . . . This is not going to end well."

AGENT DAWN: That's because he knew you were trouble. Who shows up to a first date on a motorcycle? And you made fun of our names. You really make a great first impression, babe.

AGENT MARCO: He named his first daughter after himself! I've never heard of anyone doing that! It's funny!

AGENT DAWN: It's endearing!

AGENT COOPER: Can we get back to Grandpa, please?

AGENT MARCO: Here's the truth, bud. Don was blunt to the point of being rude. He never really liked me, but he loved my mother's lemon meringue tarts, so he let me stick around. Plus, you know, your mom was so smitten with me, she knew she couldn't live without me.

AGENT DAWN: Don't listen to your father. Grandpa was just very straightforward. But you're right about the tarts. He definitely liked those tarts more than you.

AGENT COOPER: Was he in the army? Was he a paratrooper?

AGENT DAWN: He really didn't talk about his past. You know, I always assumed he was a Vietnam deserter.

AGENT MARCO: Makes sense. So anti-government. We should call the Feds and hand him over!

AGENT DAWN: I'd consider handing you over first, your biggest crime being that you hog the remote.

AGENT COOPER: Was he into skydiving?

AGENT DAWN: Skydiving? How is anyone "into" skydiving? I can't imagine anything worse. Ooh! A new episode of *The Great British Bake Off!* Marco, put that one on. You can check the game on the commercials.

At this point the interview was halted for reasons

beyond Agent Cooper Arcano's control, as the
ensuing argument between pie and puck became
heated. However, the nugget of information that
Don Cooke may have been in the army and may
have been a paratrooper is definitely key to this
investigation.

END MISSIVE

Before class the next day, Ali came up to me. He
held up a Batman comic in a large plastic bag.

"Look," he said. "It says 1955. I looked it up online. It's a big one. Not a million dollars, but maybe
a thousand. Imagine if we got a thousand bucks?"

"That would be cool," I admitted.

"Think of what we could buy," Ali said.

I wanted to bring up the bet again, but I could
tell that Ali didn't want to talk about it. So we stood
there awkwardly.

"Did you see that video yesterday of the dog sav-
ing the rabbit from the river?" I finally asked.

Ali smiled. "Yeah! He totally looked like Dana
Scully! Oh, and I watched this awesome mash-up
of *X-Files* clips last night. It's so good!" Ali started
describing the video and we both relaxed. I didn't
know why I had been so worried. Tristan wouldn't
take my place. No one our age had even heard of
The X-Files. Ali and me, we were two of a kind.
Right?

CHAPTER 9

The next Sunday I jumped in the car before my mom had time to even register that I was there. I had a plan.

"You seem excited about visiting," she remarked. Her eyes narrowed. "Why?"

"No reason," I responded, doing up my seat belt.

"No, really. Why?"

"No. Reason. I'm just glad to be a comfort to my family members." Which I shouldn't have said. It was too over-the-top.

But I *was* excited to go back. I wanted the chance to look through Grandpa's shelves. I was hoping that a clue to his real identity would be hidden somewhere. A photo of him in the army? Maybe wearing a parachute? Or something even bigger — like a photo of him jumping out of a plane holding $200,000 in cash. This last one was a long shot but dream big and expect small, I figured.

When we got there, Grandpa was in front of the TV in the common room, nowhere near his room.

I knew I needed to get in there to get the evidence I needed to make my case.

"Hi, Dad!" Mom put on her loud, overly high and perky voice that she reserved for stressful situations. "It's me, Dawn. Your daughter!"

"I know," he grumbled. He shook his head in my direction. "Who's the kid?"

"My son, Cooper. He's your grandson." Mom pulled me into a side hug with one arm, but I pulled away quickly. I didn't want to be part of their conversation. I had things to do!

"I'm just going to the washroom," I announced to no one in particular. I started to head down the hall toward Grandpa's suite.

"It's right there," Mom said, pointing at the washroom door. "Where are you going?"

I hesitated. "Umm . . . I need more privacy. I thought I would use the one in Grandpa's room."

"Don't be ridiculous, Cooper. You can use the main one. No one's going to hear you. Or care if they do," she said.

I looked down the hall, then at Grandpa, even though I knew he would be no help. He was grumbling about the lunch being terrible, and something about bananas. Things I didn't care about, especially since I knew his photo albums could hide information of international significance.

"Fine." I stalked over to the washroom and locked the door. At least I could plan my next move in peace there.

How could I get into Grandpa's room? I needed at least ten minutes to look through the albums to see if there was anything worthwhile, maybe even fifteen.

It would be best if I could be alone, but maybe I could play on Mom's nostalgia to get her on board. I hated to do this, knowing she was stressed out already, but now that she was trying to scrapbook, she was keen to head down memory lane. The only problem was that I needed information from before her birth, information that she didn't have.

Just as I jumped up on the counter to think it through, a knock on the bathroom door pulled me out of my planning mode.

"Are you almost done in there? I'd like the opportunity to use the loo!" a familiar voice called out. Mrs. Kim! I had a brilliant idea.

"Yeah, just a sec," I called back. I flushed the toilet and ran the sink for a couple of seconds to keep up the bathroom ruse. I opened the door grandly.

"Good afternoon, Mrs. Kim!" I said.

She looked surprised, and a little worried. "Oh! Oh dear. That was quite a fright. What an overwhelming way to enter a washroom!"

"Sorry, Mrs. Kim. I didn't think you would be so close by," I responded. "Do you remember me? I'm Cooper. We've met a couple of times."

She shook her head. "Oh dear. I don't really remember. I'm so sorry. Cooper, you said? I have a touch of the Alzheimer's, you see. My husband drops me here each week for a little break from me. I can be quite tiresome!" She chuckled. "Now, more importantly, are you done with the loo?"

"Right! Yes, of course." I moved out of the way. "I'll be right here when you're done," I said. "Maybe we can do a little tour of the place."

Mrs. Kim smiled. "That sounds just lovely!"

Mom was giving me a look from across the room, so I went over to her and Grandpa.

"Um, Mrs. Kim over there asked me to show her around the place. She doesn't remember where things are," I said, putting on a voice that was quiet and kind of pathetic. "Is that okay?"

I wasn't really doing anything wrong, was I? Everything I said was probably true.

"Of course," she said. "Just don't be too long. I want to be home in time to get the pork roast on."

When Mrs. Kim emerged from the washroom, I was waiting by the door. "Shall we go?"

"Go?" she asked.

"On a tour of the place," I reminded her. She nodded and smiled widely. I held out my arm like a real gentleman, and she hooked her arm into mine.

"Onwards and upwards!" she said.

"Do you work here?" she asked, as we headed down the hall toward Grandpa's room.

I laughed. "I'm not old enough! And I would rather be something cool, like an FBI agent."

Mrs. Kim laughed along with me. "I wanted to be Miss Marple when I grew up."

"Is she an FBI agent?" I asked.

"Who?"

"Miss Marple," I said.

"Oh, I wanted to be her when I grew up!" Mrs. Kim said. I decided to let it go and look it up when I got home.

We got to Grandpa's room. I felt bad going in. I hate it when I know my mom's been in my room when I'm not home. But still, a good FBI agent has to be willing to do difficult things.

"And where is this?" Mrs. Kim asked.

"This is my grandpa's room," I said. "Please, have a seat." I pointed to the chair in the corner. Thankfully, Grandpa's room was totally spotless. "I thought we could take a break here."

Mrs. Kim settled into Grandpa's chair. "I don't know if I told you this already, but I have a touch of the Alzheimer's, so my memory isn't as good as it was. Have I been here before?"

"I don't think so," I said. "But isn't the view good?" I directed Mrs. Kim's gaze to the window.

"Oh, it reminds me of Korea. I was born on Jeju Island. It's very beautiful. Have you been?"

"To Korea?" I asked. "No."

"Jeju is very beautiful." Mrs. Kim started talking about oranges and tangerines and eating raw abalone straight from the sea (which sounds gross; I hate seafood).

I was listening to her, but also pulling out photo albums and flipping through them.

There wasn't much there. One whole album was photos of my mom and Auntie Jane as kids. My grandma was also in a lot of photos. I never really knew her, since she died when I was five. One thing that did strike me was that Grandpa was rarely in any of the pictures. I wondered if he was trying to avoid having his picture taken in case someone recognized him as D.B. Cooper.

I pulled a few more albums off the shelf and was flipping through them when I noticed that Mrs. Kim was silent. I looked up, and she was staring at me.

"Sorry? I got distracted," I said.

"Why are you snooping?" she asked. "We're in a stranger's room, and you're going through all their things, and I just don't know what we're doing here, unless you're a thief! In fact, I believe that the best thing to do is call the staff!" She had raised her voice.

"No, no. Mrs. Kim! I promise I'm not a thief. This isn't a stranger's room. It's my grandfather's. I said that. He lives here, I swear. I'll introduce you two. I'm not snooping. I just really wanted to show you . . ." I searched hastily through the photo album in my hand ". . . this. I thought you would like to see this, um, this photo of me as a kid."

I showed her the book and pointed to me and Mom and Grandpa.

Mrs. Kim looked skeptical but glanced at the photo. "I know this place. Where is it?"

"I think it's in Ladner? Probably Westham Island. I don't know, but we used to go there a lot."

She smiled. "We used to take my niece there to feed the ducks."

"Yeah, that's what we used to do too. My grandpa used to make up bird calls. He does a really good impression of Donald Duck."

"I love ducks," Mrs. Kim said.

Talking about the ducks at Westham Island reminded me of the last time we went there, a few years ago, and Grandpa told Mom about the Alzheimer's diagnosis. They had given me three bags of food to keep me busy, but it was hard to care about feeding all the ducks with Mom crying and Grandpa trying to comfort her. I remembered how I almost got bit by a goose who charged over to get the bags from my hand.

"He looks like someone famous, doesn't he?" Mrs. Kim asked, still looking at the picture.

"Actually, I think he was famous," I said. "But I don't think anyone knows that."

She smiled conspiratorially. "That sounds mysterious. I love mysteries."

I debated whether I should tell her my theory or not. Finally, I gave in. "I think he's D.B. Cooper. The skyjacker from the seventies," I said.

"That's so nice!" she said. "Have you ever been a skyjacker?"

"No, I've never been a skyjacker. That would mean I would be either dead or in jail."

Mrs. Kim looked confused. "Sorry, dear. What's a skyjacker?"

"It's a guy who hijacks a plane," I explained.

Now Mrs. Kim looked shocked. "That's a crime!"

"Oh, totally. It's a big one. But I think he hijacked a plane back in the seventies. He demanded a bunch of money and some parachutes. They actually gave it to him and he jumped out of the plane and he's been hiding in Canada. No one else knows, not even my mom. I'm going to prove it."

"So he's a terrorist?" Mrs. Kim asked.

I wanted to get mad but I glanced at Mrs. Kim, and she was looking at me very innocently. I thought about her question. It never seemed like he was a terrorist.

"Well, he didn't kill people," I reasoned. "Well, I mean, he threatened to . . . but . . . but he wouldn't have done it . . . From everything I read, he was really nice about it. I don't think he was serious." I was confused. D.B. Cooper wasn't a terrorist. He just wanted money. That's different, isn't it?

"I have to go," I said abruptly to Mrs. Kim. "We should return you to the main room."

She stood up slowly and reached for my arm. "Well, then, let's be off. You have to lead the way. I have no idea where to go!" She chuckled to herself.

I took her arm and dropped her off in the main room at a table with an empty seat. Mom was sitting next to Grandpa, both of them watching a random cooking show. I bet they never changed the channel at this place. Mom had her notebook open. I peeked at it over her shoulder. There were just some doodles underneath today's date. Mom looked up at me and smiled when I perched on the arm of her chair. Grandpa didn't even look at me.

"Have you been watching TV the whole time?" I asked.

"Shhhh." Grandpa shot me a glare.

Mom nodded and whispered, "I gave up asking questions today. It's just not the right time. I think I'm the only one here who has any idea what they're making on this show though."

"Which is?" I whispered back.

"Soufflés," she said, then she laughed a little. "Actually, even I don't know. I haven't been paying attention."

We sat there until the end of the program, the three of us, silently.

On the way home I started thinking about our trips to Westham Island again.

"Did we go to Westham Island a lot with Grandpa?" I asked.

Mom looked at me, surprised. "We did, actually. We also went to Boundary Bay to try to spot owls and herons. Do you remember that?"

I shook my head. "Not really."

"Your dad loves the air show out there. We should try to go next year. It's been a while since we went. Maybe we'll do that." Mom was quiet for a moment, then laughed. "We went berry picking at Westham Island too. You were probably too young to remember. You kept eating all the strawberries out of Grandpa's bucket and then you wiped your red hands all down his white shirt and cried because you thought he had cut himself."

I laughed at the story.

"I like strawberries," I said.

"Me too." She paused. "Grandpa too."

"We should bring him some next week," I said.

She nodded. "Good idea, hon."

Mom didn't say much the rest of the way home, or the rest of the night. She and Dad moved around each other like ghosts, not arguing but not really talking either. This new behaviour felt worse. I tried to listen to them after I went to bed, but Mom went to bed early and Dad watched TV alone. Was it weird that I felt better when they were arguing than when they didn't talk to each other at all?

What if they really were getting divorced? Mom was so stressed out by Grandpa that I debated telling her my D.B. Cooper theory. Maybe if I could prove it, she wouldn't have to worry so much. We could tell Grandpa we knew, and he could move somewhere safe, and Mom and Dad could go back to being normal. They wouldn't have Grandpa to fight about anymore. Plus, I would have my hundred dollars so I could give that money to my mom to help pay for Grandpa's stuff.

But I wasn't stupid. I knew a hundred dollars wouldn't go very far. I knew what I had to do.

CHAPTER 10

On Monday I made sure to find a minute alone with Tristan. I didn't want Ali to know what I was doing.

"Tristan!" I called.

He turned around and smiled. "Hey, Coop! You should have come to Ali's yesterday. He had an epic run on *Mario Kart*."

Anger flared, knowing that they had hung out without me. "CoopER. And I couldn't come. I had to visit my grandpa."

"Too bad. It was so awesome. At first Ali chose to be Yoshi and I was like, 'Yoshi? You sure?' But then—"

I interrupted him. "Let's double the bet. Double or nothing."

"What?"

"I want to double down. Two hundred bucks," I said.

"Seriously?"

I nodded, confident in my choice.

"Why not? Yeah, sure. I could use that two hundred bucks."

I smiled. "So could I." We shook on it just as Ali walked up.

"What are you guys doing?" he asked worriedly. He looked from my face to Tristan's.

"Nothing," we both said together.

"I heard you had an epic game yesterday," I said, changing the subject.

"Oh yeah! It was amazing!"

"Yeah, so he chose Yoshi, and I was like, 'Yoshi? You sure?' But then he ramped up with a drift boost—" Tristan got really excited and started to tell me everything again. But I didn't want to hear a play-by-play of their afternoon, so I cut him off.

"What's going on with the Batman comic?" I asked Ali.

"What Batman comic?" asked Tristan.

"Just this thing Ali and I found," I said. I was glad he didn't know about it. It made me feel better.

Ali sighed. "Oh man. So I went online to see if I could get info on how much it would be worth, but it's impossible. I don't know where else to find out."

"Uh, guys? I'm going to go. Emma has the other half of our science project and she's over there," Tristan announced.

"See ya," I said, glad to see him leave, but also glad that we had upped our bet. Two hundred bucks was a pretty good amount.

It wasn't until halfway through the day that I

started to worry about my new plan. Was I sure enough I was right to put down a bunch of money I didn't have? I thought about what D.B. Cooper would have done. I mean, the guy jumped out of a plane. He wouldn't have blinked at doubling down on a stupid bet. I had to have the confidence of D.B. Cooper. It ran in the family. It was in my bones.

CASE: 0024 / File: 0003
LOCATION: Vancouver, British Columbia

Further research has indicated that hijacking a plane in the 1970s wasn't all that uncommon. There were many hijacked planes, and most of the men who hijacked them were looking for money, or going to Cuba. I have never been to Cuba, so it seems like a strange destination, although further internet research proves that it is a popular resort country for Canadians.

Due to the fact that D.B. Cooper basically hijacked the plane to get money, Agent Cooper Arcano has come to the conclusion that D.B. Cooper cannot be considered a terrorist in the same way that the guys who took over the planes on 9/11 were. Private gain is not the same as terrorism. Agent Mrs. Kim will be informed of this decision upon the next meeting.

Agent Cooper Arcano has also conducted a search of the photographic archives at both the alleged D.B. Cooper's room, and the basement of D.B. Cooper's daughter. There is little photographic evidence linking Don Cooke to D.B. Cooper, but there is also no photographic evidence proving the contrary. The only thing to do is continue looking. (Agent Cooper also noted that men's pants from the seventies is a trend he hopes never comes back.)

END MISSIVE

"What are you doing down here?"

Mom came downstairs just as I was pulling a box down from the back of the storage space in our basement.

"I'm looking for stuff about the family. For a school project," I said. I pointed to the ground, where I had started a pile of things that I thought might yield some information about Grandpa. There were only a few things there. I had found a couple of younger photos of Grandpa with Mom, Auntie Jane and Grandma, and one that looked like Grandpa standing by a giant white arch. Mom picked that one up.

"Oh, I remember when we took this photo!" she said. "Grandma tried to surprise him with a trip to Seattle for his birthday. When we got to the border, he said that Seattle was an awful place. He told us this story about getting ripped off at a bank or something? I can't remember the exact reason, but he swore up and down that he wouldn't give Seattle one more cent of his hard-earned money and he would wait for us at the Peace Arch. The Peace Arch is right at the border — do you remember passing it when we went camping a couple of years ago?" She laughed. "Grandpa was so stubborn. I still remember him saying in the car: 'They won't get one red cent, Linda. Not one.' He was insistent, but Grandma was bound and determined to go anyway."

"You guys went to Seattle and left him there?" I asked.

"No. He got out of the car and stood there smoking, so Grandma drove across the border and we sat in a parking lot in Blaine for an hour eating french fries, then we went back. There he was, still standing there, like we had only been gone a few minutes. Grandma took this picture from the car as we drove up. That's why it's blurry. She was driving and trying to focus the camera," Mom explained. She handed the photo back to me. "Why did you choose this one? It's a terrible photo."

"I wanted one of the Peace Arch. It's symbolic," I said. "Do you know if any of these other boxes have any of Grandpa's stuff in them? I was hoping for some army medals or something."

"Honey, we don't even know if he was in the army. Your grandfather was a very private person. We certainly would never have asked him questions the same way you always ask questions. My curious little monkey," she teased. She looked so sad suddenly. "It's just too bad that we won't get the answers to a lot of your ancestry questions from him. I wish I had thought about that a few years ago, before . . ."

"So I'm not going to find anything here?" I said.

"You might, but I wouldn't get your hopes up. Most of his stuff is at Auntie Elena's work. Which reminds me: I asked your father months ago to clean out space in the garage so we could get it from her and he still hasn't done it." Suddenly her mood switched. "Make sure everything's back on the shelves when you're done. I don't want to see a mess here tomorrow."

Count on moms to ruin a perfectly good research session.

Lying in bed that night, I thought about the story Mom had told me about Grandpa. Why wouldn't he go to Seattle? There was only one reason I could think of: he was a wanted man in the States. He probably wasn't allowed to cross the border, but he couldn't tell his wife why without raising suspicion. Or maybe, maybe Grandma knew! Maybe this was the moment when he knew that she knew and he thought she was trying to turn him in to the Feds!

But that didn't make sense. Why would they stay married if Grandma thought he was a skyjacker? Or if he thought she was going to turn him in? They must have really been in love. Would Mom stay married to Dad if he was a skyjacker? I doubted it. But then, I didn't know if she would stay married to him right now. I didn't like thinking about it.

I was at a dead end. I turned my pillow to the cold side and reached to pet Dana Scully, who was curled up into the corner of my bed and the wall. If we were actually detectives on *The X-Files*, what would Dana Scully be saying to Mulder right now? I knew I didn't have any answers, but I realized that I didn't even know the questions I should be asking.

"Scully, what are we missing?" I whispered into her fur. "What is the key to finding D.B. Cooper?" I lay there in bed, thinking and planning, for a long while before I could close my eyes.

Waking up, I knew what I needed. I needed one of those unsolved-mystery walls with string connecting the dots, like Fox Mulder had when his cases got too complicated.

I came home from school armed with a giant piece of posterboard I'd gotten from the librarian. On one side was a class project for emergency preparedness, but the other side was blank. It was perfect for my D.B. Cooper investigation. I could keep it flipped over to avert Mom's suspicions and pretend like I was working on the earthquake kit portion of the board.

I cleared my desk for the giant poster. I started by taking a black felt marker and writing D.B. COOPER MYSTERY SOLVED. I didn't quite plan it right, so I had to squeeze the "ed" at the end, but it looked okay. Then I taped the composite drawing of D.B. Cooper to the middle of the poster. I taped the photo of Grandpa on the right and put a giant black question mark beside it. Then I made a little box for all the information I had about Grandpa on the right side.

```
GRANDPA
born in Chicago
was an adult in 1971
moved to Canada
married to Linda Marques
two kids: Dawn and Jane
refused to go to the USA
owned sunglasses
maybe in the army?
maybe a paratrooper?
draft dodger?
```

I added in a few of the photos I got from downstairs, like the one of Grandpa by the Peace Arch, and one of him and Grandma standing outside the Vancouver airport.

On the left side, I put all the information I knew about D.B. Cooper. I tried to stick to the facts, but I ran out of those pretty quickly, so I added in some strong assumptions based on what I did know.

```
D.B. COOPER
adult in 1971
American
knew how to use an altimeter
knew how to parachute
owned sunglasses
had access to a bomb
needed money
didn't know how to tie a tie (clip-on)
good at orienteering in the woods
```

Once I had all the information on the board, I got all the push pins I had taken from the desk downstairs and put one beside each point. I stole the ends of yarn from my mom's crafting box and wrapped wool around "maybe a paratrooper?" and strung it across to "knew how to parachute." I took another colour and connected "maybe a paratrooper?" and "knew how to use an altimeter." I took a look at my board. It was looking really good. I continued. "Was an adult in 1971" was connected on both sides, and same for "American" and "born in Chicago."

Satisfied with my work, I flipped over the poster and learned about earthquake drills before allowing myself a well-deserved TV break before dinner. Next stop: getting evidence from Grandpa's room.

CHAPTER 11

I slept over at Ali's on Saturday night, which was good timing. Not just because my house felt like a ticking time bomb of arguments, but also because Tristan was visiting his grandparents for the weekend, so it was just me and Ali.

When I arrived, Ali flung the door open and hustled me inside. "Come on! I've got the best idea!"

I kicked off my shoes, and Ali practically pushed me into his room. I looked around. Ali had two bookcases full of comics and graphic novels, and they were all perfectly straight. He was crazy about keeping his comics in order. He had the pile of comics he had gotten from the library sale stacked neatly on his desk.

"I need you to help me sort these comics. If Issue 91 from 1955 is worth even $500, imagine how much money might be sitting right in front of us."

I shrugged. "Five hundred and one dollars?"

"No way! We need to look through and see if we can find any marks or rips in any of them. If there's something there, they aren't worth anything." He handed me half the pile.

"Mom also said we can order pizza for dinner," Ali said. "But we can't eat it while we look at the comics. Greasy fingerprints," he explained.

Sorting comics sounded super boring, but after a while I got into it. Most of the comics had rips or smudges, but two of them were in pretty good condition. Plus, some of the plots from the fifties and sixties were so ridiculous. One of the ones I read was all about a hot-air balloon ride. That was pretty much it.

We didn't find any others that seemed to be in as good a shape as the one Ali had already pulled out. I saw that he had it in a plastic bag sitting on top of his dresser.

I pointed to it. "Dude, you need to keep that comic in a safe place, you know. I mean, what if there was a fire or something? Or what if your sister decided that she needed money and stole it? Or your house got broken into? The guys across the street from us got broken into last summer and they took everything."

Ali looked worried. "Where should I put it? Where would you put it?"

I thought about it. "I don't actually know. I think it's fine here for now. But I'll come up with something."

Ali looked relieved. "Thanks, man. I can always count on you."

Him saying that made me smile. I was so glad to have my best friend back and not have to share him.

"I've been thinking about my bet, and I know what I'm going to do with the money when I win," I said.

"*If* you win," Ali corrected me.

"WHEN I win. I'm going to give it to my mom and dad."

"Why?" Ali looked confused.

"So they can pay bills or something. Mom's all worried about debts. Maybe this will make them like each other again."

Ali looked suspicious. "You need way more than a hundred dollars to pay bills, though."

"Two—" but I stopped myself from correcting him. I hadn't told Ali about doubling the bet. "I mean, I know. But a hundred bucks is still pretty good money."

Ali was silent for a second, then asked tentatively, "And what if you don't win?"

"I don't know," I admitted. "I could just avoid Tristan for the rest of my life, I guess."

"How? He's our friend," Ali said.

I shrugged and mumbled, "More like your friend. He's so . . . normal. I'm too weird for him."

"He's weird too, you know," Ali tried to convince me.

"I am more weird," I said. "I'm the weirdest."

"No. I am the weirdest," Ali said, talking in a robot voice and making jerky motions.

"I'm the weirdest," I cackled like a witch, and threw the damaged comics into the air.

"I'm the weirdest!" Ali shouted in an English accent, stomping around the room.

"You're both the weirdest!" we heard Ali's sister shout through the closed door, which made us both laugh so hard we couldn't see anymore.

***

I wasn't fully prepared for my reconnaissance mission at Grandpa's the next day, especially since Ali and I had stayed up watching *The X-Files* and eating pizza. So when Mom picked me up, I was shocked to see Dad in the passenger seat.

"Are we dropping you off somewhere?" I asked, as I got into the back seat of the van.

"Nope," Dad said. "I am a very loving husband and I just wanted to spend some quality time with my beautiful wife and my super smart kid and my cranky but truly loveable father-in-law who hates me but secretly respects me in a manly way."

Mom actually laughed. "Your father lost a little bet yesterday, and so he'll be joining us to visit Grandpa for the next four weeks." She turned to Dad. "I bet you wish you hadn't doubled down on the second game. It could have been twice, but you thought you could beat me."

"Your mother is a dart shark," Dad said. "Life lesson here, Cooper. Never play darts with a woman who cleans teeth for a living. She has killer aim with small pointy things. I told her that she could be a vampire hunter when we were at the pub last night."

"Hygienist by day, slayer by night," my mom announced, and they both laughed.

They hadn't been this nice to each other in ages. It was definitely not how parents who were getting divorced acted. I relaxed a little. Maybe things were going to be okay.

I was glad to have Dad there too. It would be good to have someone else to distract Mom while I snooped through Grandpa's room again. There had to be something, even something little, that would give me a hint of where to go next in my search for the truth.

Dad joked and laughed all the way to Golden Sunsets, making comments that Mom would alternately laugh at and scold him for.

"They should call this place 'Golden Dentures.' Did you see that woman's teeth? Dawn, you could make a killing offering your services here. Wait: Was 'a killing' hitting too close to home in an old folks' home?" Dad was still whispering zingers as I punched in the code at the door to Grandpa's ward.

Dad hadn't been there in so long that I think he had forgotten what it was like. He looked around at all the empty chairs and the blaring TV, then turned to me.

"Cooper, buddy. I know you love me, but if I ever end up needing to be in a place like this, I want you to shoot me, okay?"

Mom frowned. "Marco. That's not funny."

"What? I'm not trying to be funny. Look around!" Dad was happy, but Mom's attitude soured walking into Grandpa's ward.

I didn't know how to not take sides, so I turned to Mom to change the subject. "Should I go get Grandpa? It'll be too crowded in his room."

"You want to go alone?" Mom asked. "We can get a nurse to bring him out." She looked around for someone to ask.

"Mom, it's fine. If I need help, I'll press the call button. It's not a big deal," I replied. I could hear the annoyance in my own voice. I didn't want my parents to think I was a kid who always needed help. After all, I was on the verge of solving the biggest unsolved mystery the FBI had ever encountered, and Mom and Dad were the only things standing between me and the evidence right now.

"Let the kid go," Dad said. "We can go and make bets with the other patients on things that they don't remember happening. This place is a gold mine!" He laughed, oblivious to Mom's mood shift.

"You're never coming back again, Marco." She turned to me. "Make sure you hit that call button if Grandpa is being difficult. You know how challenging he can be."

"Yeah, yeah. I know. But give me a chance!" I said. "You don't have to come running thirty seconds from now. We'll be back. Make yourselves comfortable."

I pointed to the chairs closest to the hallway.

Dad gave me a salute and sank into one of the chairs, while Mom propped herself up on the chair arm next to him. She said something to him that I couldn't hear, and he groaned.

"It doesn't mean anything," I whispered to myself. I didn't have time to think about the state of their marriage. I had a mystery to solve to make it all better.

CHAPTER 12

I knocked on Grandpa's open door and entered his room. He was sitting in his armchair, staring at the wall.

"Hi, Grandpa. It's Cooper," I said. "I'm your grandson. My mom is Dawn."

"Hmmh?" He startled. "My grandson?" Grandpa looked at me studiously. "Well, damn. You are the spitting image of me when I was a kid. I'm not surprised we're related."

This was off to a good start. "Oh yeah? We look like each other?" Mom had always said that we had the same eyes, but I looked more closely at him. His hair was straight and thin, like mine, except mine was dark brown. And the same eyebrows. I guessed he was kind of right.

"Like looking in a . . ." he said.

"Mirror." I helped him with the word.

"I know. Mirror. I know. How old are you?"

"Twelve," I said. Then I thought I would test the waters a little. "How old are you?"

90

"Too damn old," he responded. I laughed, and he almost smiled at me. "What's your name?"

"Cooper," I said.

"Good name. Solid. What do you like?"

"What do I like to do? Oh, um. Draw? Play games?" I said.

"Games, eh? I don't know any games." He paused.

"What did you like as a kid, Grandpa? What kinds of things did you do?"

"That was a long time ago. I don't know," he said. There was another long pause. "Don't get old. It's a terrible thing."

"I'll do my best," I said. "I know you like cards. You taught me how to play cribbage," I said. "But I don't remember the rules anymore."

"Huh." He didn't seem to know what I was talking about. "Baseball. I like that baseball one."

I was onto something. He was remembering things! The secret agent in me knew this was my chance, but I was going to have to play it real smooth.

"Did you like jumping? Like off a dock into a lake or something? I like jumping into water," I said.

"Water." He repeated after me, almost like he didn't know what the word meant. But I pressed on.

"Do you like cars? Or trucks? Vehicles?"

"Yeah sure. Cars are fine."

"What about . . . airplanes?" I slid the question in smoothly.

He snorted. "Airplanes. Useful." He stressed the word, elongating it as he thought about what it meant. That's when I knew for sure. He had to be talking about the skyjacking! What else is a plane that useful for?!

"Takes a lot of money to travel by plane now," I said. "I bet you wish you had a lot of money."

Grandpa looked at me then like I was the stupidest kid he'd ever met. "Boy, everyone wishes they had a lot of money." Under his breath, he muttered a swear word. I'd blown it. One question too far. I waited a few moments, scuffing my sneakers against the carpet.

"My mom and dad are waiting for us in the common room. Do you want to come out and see them?" I asked after a bit of time had passed.

"I don't know who you're talking about," he said.

"My mom, Dawn. And my dad is Marco. Dawn is your daughter," I reminded him.

"What the hell are you doing in my room?" he asked. He looked so angry that I thought someone had come in the room behind me, so I turned around. It was still just me.

"I came to get you," I said. "Mom wanted to visit you."

Grandpa stared at me. "Get out," he said. "Get out of my room." His voice was low but threatening.

"Grandpa, I'm Cooper. I'm your grandson," I said. I put my hands up in mock surrender. "I'm on your side."

"GET OUT!" he yelled. He stood up. "GET OUT NOW!"

His demeanour had changed so fast I didn't see it coming. I stumbled backwards toward the door, but I knocked into the short bookcase beside the frame. The lamp sitting on top of the bookcase wavered and fell, and the base broke into several pieces.

"What are you doing?!" Grandpa roared.

I scrambled onto my hands and knees, trying to pick up the pieces of the lamp. "I'm so sorry, Grandpa. I'm really sorry." I was panicking now.

"You broke my . . . my . . . that's my . . ." Grandpa was angry and struggling for the right word.

"What's going on in here?" Dad was at the door behind me.

"This kid broke my . . . my . . ." Grandpa still didn't know what it was, but Dad cut him off.

"Your lamp? Cooper, why are you breaking lamps?" Dad's tone was soft and soothing, not the joking voice he normally had. He bent down and picked up the lampshade from beside me, then put his hand under my elbow, guiding me back up to my feet. He left his hand on my shoulder and squeezed it gently.

"He has to pay for that . . ." Grandpa paused to remember the word, standing his ground and pointing at the broken bits in my hand. Most of his bluster had left him.

Dad pulled out his wallet. "The lamp? Yeah

sure, Don. We can pay for the lamp. How much does Cooper owe you? Will five bucks do?" Dad turned and winked at me.

Grandpa looked flustered. He blinked several times. "No. No, it's more than that."

Dad pulled out a five and a ten-dollar bill and held them out for Grandpa to take. "Fifteen good? Can't be more than fifteen."

Grandpa looked at the bills in Dad's hand and shook his head. "That's not real money. You can't pander to me with your damn play money. Green . . . skins. Real money is green." He was starting to get riled up again. I looked at Dad and got ready to hit the call button, but he looked calm and was leaning casually on the door frame.

"Right. The American stuff. You drive a hard bargain, Don. I've only got a green twenty. You have change?"

Grandpa looked at it closely, then grumbled. "Yeah. Yeah. I got change," he said. He put his hand in his back pocket and pulled out his wallet. He opened it up, and I gasped.

Normally when he gave me a dollar, it looked like it was the only bill in his wallet. But this time he pulled out a wad of American bills, old ratty ones all held together with a blackened old elastic band.

Dad whistled. "Whoa, Don. Where did you get that kind of money?"

Grandpa snapped his wallet closed and shoved it down the side of his armchair.

"None of your business. Never mind. None of your business. Never mind." Grandpa snatched the twenty from Dad's hand and sat back down in his armchair, stuffing his wallet under the cushion then sitting on it.

I looked at Dad to see what he'd do next. He raised his eyebrows at me and shrugged.

"Well, Don. Always a pleasure to see you. Take care of yourself," Dad said, saluting as he turned away.

"Um, bye, Grandpa," I said as we left.

There was no response.

CHAPTER 13

"I swear, Dawnie, the guy is sitting on a gold mine. There had to be a few hundred in that bundle, maybe even a grand!" Dad turned around, straining against his seat belt to see me. "I'm right, eh, Cooper? The old man is LOADED."

"It's true, Mom. I saw it too," I agreed.

"And I bet he has more hidden away in that little room. I bet if you could just get in there without him, you'd find all sorts of little secrets," Dad said.

"I can't believe you didn't call the nurse to come and work with him. You can't let him get worked up like that. He was a bear to deal with when I went in."

After Dad and I left Grandpa's room, Mom went in to visit him alone for a short while, leaving Dad and me out in the common area to fend for ourselves. I looked around for Mrs. Kim — I even left to see if she was out in the garden or by the door — but I couldn't find her anywhere. When I came back, Dad had changed the channel on the

TV to football and dragged two of the overstuffed chairs closer, creating a little couch and footrest for himself. When Mom came out, I could tell that she wanted to yell at him, but instead she just pulled the chair out from under his feet and put it back in the corner where it had been.

"We're going," she announced.

It was a long drive home. Mom's good mood going to Golden Sunsets had been replaced with worry for Grandpa and annoyance with Dad (although I wasn't sure which emotion she was feeling more), and Dad wasn't making things any better by talking about Grandpa's money.

But I knew where the money came from. It looked old and ripped, straining against the tatty elastic holding the bundle together. If my theory was right, then Dad was also right: there would be other bundles of money around Grandpa's room.

As soon as we got home, I took Dana Scully out for a super long walk, hoping to avoid the big blow-up fight I was sure was coming. And I was successful, kind of. When I got back, Mom was putting on her shoes. She looked up at me and her eyes were rimmed with red. She had changed out of her contacts to her glasses already.

"I'm heading to Marilyn's house," she said. "Pick up next month's book for book club. Your dad is in charge of dinner." She shuffled past me on the landing, where I was taking off Dana's leash, and then she leaned over and kissed the top of my head.

"Try to go to bed early tonight, okay? I can only assume you were up late last night, and you have school tomorrow." I nodded mutely, not really sure if I should say something or not.

Mom left, and I went into the kitchen. Dad was moving around, agitated. He didn't seem to have any purpose; he was opening and closing cupboards and drawers like he would find something hidden in them but wasn't actually looking for anything.

"What are you doing?" I asked.

"Men's pizza night?" he answered without looking at me. His voice was kind of weird and shaky.

"Sure," I said. "I'm going to work on stuff in the computer room." I did not want to be in the same room as him.

"Sure. I'll put the order in. Pepperoni? I'm going to clean up the garage. Listen for the doorbell, okay?"

I watched the door close behind him and felt tears starting to form. I swallowed them back and went into the computer room. Crying wouldn't help. Solving this case would.

CASE: 0024 / FILE: 0004
LOCATION: Vancouver, British Columbia

According to calculations by Agent Cooper Arcano, D.B. Cooper was given $200,000 in cash, as per his demands on the airplane. He was also given food for the crew (that he asked for, which is pretty nice of him) and four parachutes.

In 1980 a boy found $5,800 buried close to a campground north of Portland. The money was burned and tattered and ripped, but matched the serial numbers of the bills given to D.B. Cooper nine years previous.

This means that D.B. Cooper could still have $194,200 in his possession.

Making estimations on how one would use and disseminate that money over the years, let's assume that D.B. Cooper was frugal and careful with his money.

So he only uses $2,000 a year in cash, doling it out in slow, careful wads and exchanging it into Canadian money. He also, presumably, got a job to support his new family of one wife and two kids.

So, $200,000 in 1971

minus $2,000 a year for 45 years (for a total of $90,000)

leaves him with $110,000

minus the $5,800 found by the boy

and assuming a margin of error of $1,000, because no one is perfect

means that D.B. Cooper could have around $103,200 hidden in his room!

(Agent Cooper also noted that if math problems were this interesting in school, he would probably have done better at solving them.)

END MISSIVE

I realized that winning this bet meant a lot more than two hundred dollars. If Grandpa was sitting on a hundred thousand dollars, he could totally pay his own bills and Mom wouldn't have to worry about paying for the care home.

I smiled. That money would solve everything. Mom and Dad could pay all their bills and like each other again. Grandpa would be fine, and maybe even give some money to us to go on a cool vacation. I would get Tristan's money from our bet and spend it on getting really good comics for me and Ali, and we'd be best friends forever. I didn't know why people said money wasn't everything. It sure seemed like it would make life a lot easier.

***

The next morning I remembered that I was supposed to find a safe place for Ali's comic book.

"Did you get your book?" I asked Mom while she was making lunches.

"Hmmm? Oh, right. Sorry I wasn't home for bedtime. Did you get to bed at a reasonable hour at least?"

"Of course." I put two slices of bread in the toaster and leaned on the counter to wait for them to brown.

"If you had something that was really valuable, would you keep it at home?"

"No, we have a safety deposit box," she said.

"Did Grandpa have a safety deposit box?" I asked.

"Your grandpa? No way. Everything he had that was valuable he kept at home. There was this fire-proof filing cabinet in the den that we never opened. Still haven't. We never found the keys." She put down her mustard-covered knife and looked at me. "Does this have to do with Grandpa's money? Your dad was kidding yesterday. You know that, right? Grandpa doesn't have wads of cash. Trust me."

"It's not about Grandpa," I insisted. "Ali and I were talking about comic book original editions, and I was just thinking about where we could keep them. It's not a big deal. Forget I said anything."

I finished off my toast, then grabbed my back-pack. "See you later," I said, taking my lunch bag off the counter.

"Cooper! I've picked up a shift, so I'll be late home tonight!" Mom called after me. "But your dad will be home by four."

"Okay," I said. "Bye! Bye, Scully!"

"Learn something interesting!"

Little did she know that I already had. It was very possible that instead of having all the cash in his room, Grandpa had a locked filing cabinet of secrets. And I bet that if I got the key, I could find out way more about Grandpa than he ever wanted anyone to.

Ali's comic book was going to have to wait.

Of course, I couldn't get that key for another week *and* I had to figure out where he would keep it. I spent the bus ride mentally going through

Grandpa's room, thinking of all the small places where he could've hidden stuff. I made a list during English of all the places I could look and categorized them into three groups.

CASE: 0024 / FILE: 0005
LOCATION: Vancouver, British Columbia

An overview of Room 305, Don Cooke's room, for attempts to find a hidden key or wad of $103,000 in American cash.

Secret Hiding Places in Plain Sight (Easy to Check)

- top of bookcase, inside brass spittoon full of change

- top of bookcase, under mallard-duck statue

- middle of bookcase, behind Norman Rockwell decorative plates

- inside plant holder shaped like a turkey with no legs

- taped to back of TV (unlikely, but you never know!)

Real Secret Hiding Places (Medium to Check)

- behind the "A Round Tuit" decorative plate on the wall (tough to get off the wall, if I ever get around to it!)

- inside a *National Geographic* magazine on the bookshelf (too many to go through quickly!)

- down the sides of Grandpa's armchair, or under

the butt cushion (Grandpa's always sitting there!)

- inside the frame of the family portrait (like in that movie that I can't remember the name of, but it was good!)

- inside the fake Fabergé egg beside the TV (have to break it to look inside!)

- in one of the boxes in the closet (how to explain going through the closet to my mom?)

Super Secret Hiding Places (Too Hard or Gross to Check)

- bottom of the underwear drawer

- inside dirty laundry hamper

END MISSIVE

I decided to check the first list that coming Sunday, and if I could, I would try to get into the shoeboxes on the top shelf of Grandpa's closet. Hopefully, I could find a key.

CHAPTER 14

After lunch with Ali and Tristan — who only talked about soccer the whole time, despite my attempts to change the subject to something I knew stuff about — we had drama class together.

Normally, I kind of hate drama — having to get up in front of each other and pretend stuff. I can never tell if I'm supposed to get really into it or if I should play it cool, and every time it's my turn I seem to choose wrong and then all the kids laugh. Plus, my face turns red so fast no matter what, and I'm always way sweatier than normal and I look really embarrassed, mostly because I am embarrassed. I only took it because my mom told me it would be fun, but next year I am definitely taking something else as my option class, like coding or Japanese.

Today wasn't terrible though; in fact, the class was very useful for getting in the heads of the people involved in my case. Ms. Patrick wanted us to do a guided meditation, so she had the class lie on the floor with the lights off and our eyes closed.

"Get into the heads of your characters," she said. "I want you to feel what they feel. Pick a character from your favourite story or movie. Really picture them. Imagine yourself becoming them. Your body is morphing, changing to fit this new body. Feel your bones stretching, elongating into this new person. Breathe into this new character. How do you feel? What is on your mind?" She spoke quietly, breathily. At first, I thought I would be Fox Mulder and try to solve my case. But being Fox Mulder wasn't working. Instead, I tried something else. I decided to become D.B. Cooper. I could feel the dark sunglasses perched on my nose, the dark suit, the tie constricting my neck. I pictured the thick raincoat covering my shoulders and the weight of my briefcase, ten times heavier than it had ever been before.

"Once you've grown into your character, stand up. Take a walk, silently, around the room as this new person. How does this person walk? What is their focus?"

One by one, the class stood up, still partially hidden in the dim light, and started walking. I passed by Tristan, who casually knocked my arm. I knew he was trying to get my attention but I didn't look at his face.

I was focused on being D.B. Cooper. I could feel the nervousness of what I was about to do coursing through my veins, but I was cool on the outside. I walked with purpose around the room and thought about what I was about to do. I was going to leave all the terrible things in my life behind and move forward. I was about to walk onto that plane and demand what was rightfully mine. I pictured carrying my plane ticket in one hand and a briefcase with a secret in the other hand.

"Now that you've walked for a bit, think about how you interact with others. What does your voice sound like? Do you meet people head-on or are you more timid? Greet the people you walk past, and if you feel a connection to them, have a short conversation. Introduce yourself if you want. But keep moving," Ms. Patrick intoned.

I knew I wasn't going to stop to talk to anyone today. Tristan stopped right in front of me at one point, grinning and rubbing his fingers and thumb together, like he was holding a bunch of money. I stared at him like he was an annoying mosquito. I had a plan, and no one was going to get in the way of that plan. I made eye contact with Ali, who chuckled a little and said hello in his normal voice but I didn't respond. I didn't have time for friends today. Today, D.B. Cooper was all business. I tried to avoid most people but when I couldn't, I just said hello and kept moving. I felt powerful and confident; I was the only one who knew that I had a bomb in my briefcase and I knew I would get what I wanted today. No one could stop me today.

"Now, start slowing down. Stay with your character but take a seat. When you feel ready, lie down and close your eyes again." Ms. Patrick had to speak a little louder to get over the din of the conversations happening. Most students sat down right away but I was coursing with energy. I kept going, avoiding the people who had already sat down. *D.B. Cooper doesn't sit on the ground, I thought. D.B. Cooper has places to be. D.B. Cooper is becoming a new person today. D.B. Cooper is starting a new life.* I kept walking.

"Everyone should be lying down right now," Ms. Patrick said softly. She was looking straight at me, but I stared her down. I didn't want to sit. I didn't want to go back to being Cooper Arcano. I liked being D.B. Cooper. I kept walking, making my circles around the room wider and wider. Ms. Patrick came up behind me and placed her hand on my shoulder. "Everyone needs to be lying down now," she repeated.

I looked at her and sat down, then lay down and shut my eyes.

"Now breathe deeply," she said. "Let your own personality return. Feel your bones returning to their proper places. Let your character go back to where they came from. Remember them but let them go."

Ms. Patrick's words were soft and eventually I felt like old Cooper again.

***

When Sunday came around, I was ready to start my hunt for the key to Grandpa's filing cabinet. I even filled my pockets with things I thought would be useful: a couple of bobby pins I stole from my mom's bathroom drawer (good for picking locks, according to TV); some chewing gum (in case I had to stick something open); a sheet of green dot stickers I found in the junk drawer (handy for marking spots that needed more intense inspection); leftover keys from the junk drawer that didn't look like they went with anything anymore (good as replacement keys if I found what I was looking for); and my notepad and a pen (every good agent takes notes of anything out of the ordinary).

At noon I made lunch (ham-and-cheese sandwiches with a side of dill pickles) and I set the table. I figured if nothing else, I could be a good son at the same time as asking for what I wanted. It would maybe help with the tension at home.

I went into the living room, where Mom was reading and Dad was on his tablet.

"Lunch is ready," I announced.

"Wow! What did we do to deserve this?" Mom exclaimed, putting her book on the coffee table.

"More like, What did he do? Is something broken somewhere? Are you sucking up to gain brownie points?" Dad ruffled my hair as he walked past.

"No," I said. "I'm just a good kid, trying to do something good for his wonderful parents."

Dad laughed. "Riiight. Now I really want to know what you did."

"Marco, be nice. We just got a good kid," Mom said, but as she walked past me into the kitchen she spoke out of the side of her mouth: "You can tell me about whatever it is later."

"I didn't do anything. I was hungry and I wanted something to eat before we went to Grandpa's."

Mom sighed deeply as she bit into her sandwich. Even Dad was quiet. Everything was weirdly quiet, as if I'd said something wrong.

"You don't have to go, you know," Dad said. "He won't know if you skip a week."

"You're right. Maybe we all need a little break this week. The rain's made the roads slick anyway." Mom smiled at Dad. They seemed to be getting along better today but how could she choose this week of all weeks to not go to Golden Sunsets?

"What? No! We have to go!" I said.

Both Mom and Dad looked at me.

"Wait. What?" Dad said. "You're getting a free pass and you *want* to go to see Don?"

I didn't know what to say. I needed an excuse to get there, but I couldn't tell them the truth. How would that look? *Uh, Mom, I need to see Grandpa so I can rifle through his stuff to see if I can find a key to his filing cabinet so that I can break into his secret things and see if he's the most wanted man in America for the last fifty-some years?* That wasn't going to go over well.

"It's just that . . . that . . . well, I promised Mrs. Kim I would lend her a book that we had talked about. I need to see her," I tried.

Dad laughed. "You told a lady with memory

problems that you would lend her a book? I think that can probably wait a week."

Mom looked skeptical. "Why would you lend her a book? What book? When did you tell her this? I didn't think she was even there last week."

Fail number one. I tried a more guilt-ridden approach. "I just promised I would lend it to her. You know, my book on UFOs from the Time-Life series that I got at the book sale. You said I should honour my promises. We don't have to go for that, if you don't want." I paused for effect while I built up the rest of my response. "I guess I just thought we would go, since the doctor said that routine is really good for him, didn't she? We don't need to go for long." I didn't know if the doctor had said this, but I took a chance on what I sort of knew about Alzheimer's and went from there.

Mom sighed, even deeper this time. "You're right. I should stop being lazy and just go."

Dad looked at me quizzically. "Why do I still think that you've done something wrong?"

I looked at him wide-eyed, trying to look as innocent as possible. "I swear that I'm just a good kid," I said.

He rolled his eyes. "Yeah right. Don't forget: you're still related to me. You can't be all good."

CHAPTER 15

Mom and I left Dad to clean up after lunch and headed to Grandpa's. I was the first one to the door and punched in the code to the Alzheimer's ward. As I walked in, the nurse-receptionist looked at me suspiciously.

"You have a dog under that coat?" she asked.

"Not today!" I held out the sides of my jacket to show her. She waved me in without interest.

I looked around the common room for Grandpa. He was sitting with his back to the TV. I also spotted Mrs. Kim in the corner, playing cards with one of the aides. I went over to the table first.

"Hi, Mrs. Kim. It's Cooper," I said. "Looks like you've got a good hand for poker there."

She looked up at me and smiled. "It is a good poker hand, isn't it? Too bad we're playing some other game." She turned to the aide. "What are we playing?"

"Go fish," the aide answered.

"Go fish," she repeated to me. "I'd forgotten the

name!" She chuckled. "You'll have to excuse me, I have a touch of the Alzheimer's. Your name is Charlie though, correct?"

"Cooper," I said.

"Same letter! See, my memory's not so bad," she said. "So, to what do we owe the pleasure today, Cooper?"

The aide interrupted. "Mrs. Kim, I'll be right back. I'm just going to check on Mrs. Aker over there." He gestured to his seat. "You're welcome to take over my hand."

"Oh, I can't," I said. "I'm here visiting my grandpa. He's over there." I pointed at him.

"Cool. I'll be right back, Mrs. Kim."

I leaned over to Mrs. Kim and whispered, "I'm going to solve a mystery today."

She laughed and winked at me. "Oh, I do love a good mystery!" She whispered back, "What's the mystery?"

"I'm going to figure out my grandfather's biggest secret," I replied.

Her smile faded. "But it's his secret. Why do you need to know it?"

"Well, because I think he's really famous for pulling off the perfect crime. But I don't know for sure, and I should know. After all, I'm his grandson," I said.

Mrs. Kim looked unconvinced by my reason. "I don't know about this," she said. "Secrets are secrets for a reason."

"But you were all for it last time I was here. You said you would help me solve the mystery," I said.

"Well, I disagree with myself then," she said. "I can't remember what I think every day, you know. I don't know if I've told you this, but I have . . ."

"Alzheimer's," I finished for her.

The aide returned and picked up his cards. "I'm back." Mrs. Kim looked over, gesturing for him to wait a second.

"Well, just a touch of it," she corrected me. She studied me for a moment. "In order to solve a mystery, you need to know the motive. Why did the person do what they did? Know that, and you'll know what happened." She reached up and patted my cheek. "You're a nice boy. Now I have to finish my game." She looked at her cards and put them all down with a flourish. "I have a straight!" she announced.

I picked up her cards and put them back in her hands. "You're playing go fish," I reminded her.

Mom had her notebook out again and was trying for the third time to fill it. It was a waste of time, but not for the reasons she might think. Grandpa couldn't tell her his past; he was a criminal back then!

I glanced at the show playing in the background. I was in luck. It was *The Great British Bake Off* — Mom's favourite show! And it often played with no commercials, so once she gave up on asking questions, I was sure she would get hooked learning the secret to making the perfect macaron. This was my chance to sneak off to Grandpa's room for quite a while before she noticed I wasn't there.

I headed down the hallway, praying that nobody would ask me what I was doing. The door to Grandpa's room was closed. I looked around carefully, then opened the door just enough to slip inside. I closed it quietly behind me and surveyed my surroundings.

Grandpa's room looked like it had just been cleaned. I opened the top drawer in his dresser, revealing neat lines of socks and underwear. I closed it, making a mental note to check it last, if I really had to. I opened the other two drawers, noting only perfectly folded pants and a few T-shirts. Grandpa really didn't have a lot of clothes to choose from. I ran my hand underneath the piles of clothes, feeling for anything that would be hidden under the drawer liners, but it was nothing but smooth all the way along. Well, it was a start.

I moved my search along, picking up the things on his bookcase and checking underneath everything. Nothing was taped to the bottom of his few knick-knacks. Strike two.

I was getting a bit frustrated, but I knew that I had to persevere. I had limited time and a lot of ground to cover. I stopped. What would Mulder and Scully do if this was an X-File? I closed my eyes. *If I were actually D.B. Cooper and hiding something, where would I put it?*

I thought about all the things I knew about Grandpa and D.B. Cooper while I looked inside his closet. I couldn't reach the stacked shoeboxes on the top shelves, which was really annoying. I flipped through his button-down shirts and the few jackets and coats hanging in a row. On the ground were two pairs of shoes and another shoebox. I opened the box, but it was full of papers and receipts. No key, nothing of note. I pulled out my notebook, but I had nothing to report, so I put it away again.

Time was running out. I was pushing the limits of my mom noticing that I wasn't talking to Mrs. Kim anymore, and I couldn't trust the aide not to point out the direction I'd gone in after I left the table. *Think, Cooper, think!*

I wished I had brought my list of places to look, and not just left it at home. That was a rookie move on my part. I tried to picture it while I ran my hand over and under all the surfaces in the room. I thought back to our exercise in drama. I breathed deeply, picturing myself as D.B. Cooper. I took the A Round Tuit plate off the wall: nothing there. I tried to take a few of the *National Geographics* off the bookshelf, but they were tightly squeezed in and I knew I didn't want to fight to put them back after.

I looked in the (thankfully empty) laundry hamper, but there was nothing. I swished around the contents of the spittoon, but it was only change and a button picturing me in my grade two baseball uniform. I rattled the Fabergé egg by my ear, but there was no sound from inside.

I knew I had to give up. I looked under the mallard-duck statue one more time. I opened up the top drawer — the underwear drawer — and ran my hand under the socks. I stopped when I got to the underwear side. I couldn't do it. I did not want to touch my grandpa's underwear. That was going too far. Even Fox Mulder wouldn't touch someone's underwear.

I was done. I was out. I pushed my hand down on top of the socks in frustration but my pinkie hit something hard. I stopped and pushed down again. There was definitely something underneath my hand.

I pulled open the drawer as far as it would go and felt around. There was a pair of white sports socks balled up in line with all the other white socks. I pulled the socks apart. Inside there was a small envelope. And inside the envelope?

Two small keys.

CHAPTER 16

I hit the jackpot! I stuffed the keys in my pocket and re-balled the socks, placing them right back where I'd found them. Then I slid out of Grandpa's room, running into Mom just as I was closing the door.

"What are you doing?" she asked.

"I thought you guys were in there," I stammered.

"So, you went in and we weren't there, so you . . . thought we were playing hide-and-seek? What's going on, Cooper?"

I laughed loudly, as though her hide-and-seek comment was the most hilarious thing. "Good one, Mom," I said.

"Seriously, Cooper. What were you doing?"

I stopped laughing. "Nothing."

"What were you doing in there? Tell me." She crossed her arms, and I knew I had to think faster.

"Well, I thought you were in there, and then you weren't but there was a *National Geographic* open on Grandpa's chair and it looked really interesting. I got caught up in reading it," I said.

Mom stared at me. "You were reading an old *National Geographic*?" She looked skeptical.

"Well, looking at the photos. They have good photos," I said. "It was an article on a cool place in Africa." They always had articles on Africa.

She shook her head at me and muttered, "You are your father's son," which was a comment I didn't really understand. But she seemed to accept my explanation.

"Are we going already?" I asked. "I don't mind staying."

"No, we're going," she said. "Did you give Mrs. Kim the book?"

"What book?" I asked.

"The one you were adamant about lending to her. The UFO book." Mom sounded exasperated.

"Oh. No. I totally forgot it at home. Call it a case of Sometimer's disease," I joked.

"Not funny, Cooper," she said.

"A little funny, Mom," I said.

***

That night I pulled out the keys I had kept in my pocket all day and studied them. They were small, smaller than my house keys, and looked similar to the key for my bike lock.

They matched each other, or at least it looked that way, with a silver bottom and a heavier black plastic casing on the top of the key. They were attached to a thin loop of wire.

They had to fit a filing cabinet. These must be

the keys Mom couldn't find! So now, I just had to get to the filing cabinet.

I put them in my nightstand drawer, hidden under a book in case someone was looking through my stuff quickly, turned off the light, and lay looking at the ceiling, hoping for some inspiration on where to head next.

**

"Why don't we ever go to Auntie Elena's?" I asked Mom at breakfast the next morning.

"What made you think of Auntie Elena?" Mom asked.

"She was in my dream," I lied. Well, not technically. I had been thinking about her at night, so I'm sure she carried over into my REM state.

"I've always wondered about dreams. I often remember my dreams. Like, last night I dreamed we had killer whales on the lawn."

"That's weird, Mom." We laughed. "But actually: Why don't we go to Auntie Eyeliner's?"

Mom laughed again and swatted lightly at me. "Shhh. We aren't supposed to call her that."

I called her Auntie Eyeliner because she always has on very thick, very bright eyeliner. Mom told me she is trying to achieve a "cat's eye," but it actually makes her look more like a strange bug.

"Auntie Elena is busy. She has her own life. It's different than ours. Plus, she's out in Ladner."

"So? We are out in Ladner every Sunday. And isn't Grandpa's stuff at her place?"

"Yes, some of it is at her work. For now. I have to figure out what to do with it. It's a bit of a headache though — what to keep, what to trash, what to donate. And your father is supposed to clean out our garage to make space here, which of course he hasn't done. Ugh. Thinking about it makes me tired and it's only — twenty after eight?! Cooper, we are running so late! Have you even started getting ready for school?"

I headed back upstairs and contemplated my options. There weren't many. I could try and convince Mom and Dad to go to Auntie Eyeliner's place, but I didn't know how to get from her house to her work. Plus, I didn't want to cause another big fight between them. I needed to get there without them. This was going to require some stealth. I picked up Dana Scully, who was pawing at my feet, and nuzzled her. I whispered my new secret into her ear: "Dana Scully, I'm taking this mission to Ladner."

I didn't want to go alone though. That seemed scary. I needed Ali to help me. So I asked to do some library research during silent reading and headed there with no problems. I spent time looking up maps of Ladner so that I knew where Auntie Eyeliner's garage was, and where there might be something interesting. Then I hit another jackpot. The way things were falling into place, I could tell this was all meant to be.

"Dude! You'll never guess what I found!" I slid

in next to Ali at lunch, talking fast before Tristan got to the table. "There's this awesome comic book store in Ladner and they assess the value of old comic books. We should take your Batman there!"

His eyes lit up. "Aw, yeah!" Then his face changed. "Except how would we get there?" he asked. "These are the times I wish I knew Superman."

"Are you saying you'd choose Superman as your favourite superhero?" I asked, knowing it would annoy him.

Ali scowled. "Dude. Don't even start. Super Loser Man, more like it. What I'm saying is that in THIS circumstance, and perhaps this circumstance only, it would be helpful to have Superman as your friend."

"Yeah right. You looooove Superman." He growled at me, and I laughed.

"What if we both say that we have something after school and go on Thursday?" I said.

"We'll never get there before the store closes. Plus, soccer," he countered.

I nodded and took a bite of my sandwich. "Yeah, okay." I chewed thoughtfully. "What about going on Saturday? We could say that we're going to the new Science World exhibit and get my dad to drop us off. Then we can take the SkyTrain to Richmond and catch a bus from there." I swallowed and smiled. "It's kind of a perfect plan."

Ali grinned. "These are very good ideas. I like these ideas."

Just then Tristan sat down. "What ideas?" he said excitedly.

"Nothing. Just stuff about . . . nothing." I couldn't come up with anything.

He looked a little defeated. "Oh. Okay. I thought maybe you were doing something cool."

"Not me. Ali and I aren't cool." I shrugged like it was an apology.

"Speak for yourself, dude," Ali said. "I'm very cool."

"Except that you love Superman," I argued.

"Ha!" Ali laughed sarcastically.

Tristan laughed too, a moment later. "If I could choose anyone to be on my dream soccer team, it would be Superman."

I didn't say anything, but I looked pointedly at Ali. He refused to catch my eye and changed the subject.

***

We planned out our mission on the bus home. By the time Saturday rolled around, we would be ready. I never mentioned to Ali that I had plans to leave him at the comic book store and head to Auntie Elena's garage because he didn't need to know that. He wouldn't even notice; get him in a discussion about the new X-Men comic versus the movie versions of Wolverine and I'd have trouble getting him out before dark.

That night I spent time making a birthday card for Auntie Eyeliner. I figured I would use it to suck up to her first, then I could use that to ask if I could get into Grandpa's stuff.

But that didn't seem like enough. So I made a fake letter from my teacher explaining that we had a family-tree project to complete and asking that all family members help out by granting access to all their documents and filing cabinets. I practised a signature too, using the class newsletter that was in the recycling. I printed off the letter and carefully signed Mrs. Berton's name.

I looked at my handiwork. It was pretty good. I was particularly impressed that it was a blue pen signature, so it looked like she had really signed it unless you looked closely. I folded it up and put it into one of the long envelopes from the desk drawer. I tucked the envelope inside my shirt, picked up Dana Scully and held her close to me as extra coverage, and walked brazenly past my parents sitting in the living room.

"Just going to my room!" I called to them.

"We don't care!" Dad called back.

You should, I thought. *I have illegal documents literally up my sleeve.*

Once upstairs, I tucked the keys inside the envelope and put it back in my nightstand. Now it was just a waiting game until Saturday.

CHAPTER 17

Saturday couldn't come fast enough. Ali and I had spent a lot of time planning our Ladner adventure. Neither of us had ever taken the SkyTrain without our parents. In fact, neither of us had ever gone and done stuff without a parent with us. But I'm twelve and Ali's already turned thirteen, so it was time to explore the world.

I made sure that I knew exactly where we needed to get off and what bus to take. I knew when the buses were supposed to come and where to catch the bus to come home. Then we both fed our parents the same story: There was a spy exhibit at Science World *and* an IMAX movie about beavers, and we were going to read everything and learn how to be spies. I begged, I made a case about it being during the daytime and how we'd never done anything bad, and my parents relented.

It was a good thing we had perfected our stories. My parents were okay with our solo outing, but Ali's mom called with an unexpected obstacle.

"I don't think the kids should be going. They're too young." I had picked up the extension in the den when I heard my mom say Ali's mom's name, and was listening quietly.

"I'm sure they'll be fine. We have good kids, Parveen," Mom said. I silently cheered for Mom.

"You know that kids have to be over thirteen to visit Science World without an adult," Mrs. Singh countered.

"Oh no. I didn't know that," Mom replied. "Give me a second." There was a shuffling noise as she covered the mouthpiece with her hand.

"Cooper, hang up the phone and get in here," she called. How did she know?

I hung up and walked into the kitchen. She gave me a look that I couldn't comprehend. "Did you know that you have to be thirteen?"

"Mom, age is just a number. Maturity is what counts here. And Ali is already thirteen."

"If anything goes wrong . . ." she threatened.

"It won't!" I said. She went back to the phone.

"Sorry about that, Parveen. I know you're nervous about letting them go. I'm nervous too. But Marco will drop them off and pick them up, and maybe they could take your cellphone in case they have trouble . . . I'd offer mine, but we're down to one phone these days since I dropped mine into a sink at work, long story . . . I'm sure it's fine. They're both very mature boys. They won't have a problem." She was staring intently at me like she was willing me to agree. So I nodded my head and mouthed "very mature."

She listened for a while, then repeated her phrase. "Parveen, they'll be okay. I think it's time we trust them a little. And if there is any trouble, Cooper is well aware that he would be majorly grounded. Ali knows that too, just ask him." I nodded emphatically.

"All right then . . . Marco will pick Ali up at ten on Saturday. Make sure Ali has your cellphone, and you've got Marco's number, right? They'll be just fine . . . We do have good kids . . . Yes, definitely . . . Dinner soon would be wonderful; we never did hear about your Quebec trip! All right, then. Bye."

Mom hung up and before she could say anything, I started speaking. "We won't get in trouble; we just want to see the spy exhibit. If there's a problem, we'll call you right away, but there won't be any problems because we will avoid all problems. You're the best mom ever! Can we pre-buy the tickets online? And thank you!" I kissed her on the cheek and bounded to my room, Dana Scully barking as I ran down the hallway.

***

We picked up Ali at ten Saturday morning.

Dad dropped us off in the parking lot with the specific instructions to be back in the same place at four o'clock sharp. As I got out of the van, he called me back over to the car.

"Here, buddy. Don't tell your mom I gave you this," he said, handing a twenty-dollar bill through the open window. "Buy some fries or something."

"Thanks, Dad," I said. I felt a little guilty about lying to him. He waved and pulled away, and Ali and I walked toward the entrance. We even went inside and stood in the admissions vestibule.

Ali was listing off all the snacks that his mom had packed for us, but I wanted to check for the millionth time that I had the envelope with the keys in my pack.

Why did I feel so nervous? It wasn't a big deal. We weren't even really lying about going to Science World. We picked up our online tickets and made sure to get our hands stamped for re-entry. The girl at the counter didn't even blink when we showed her the pass for two youth, so we clearly looked over thirteen. I think it's because Ali is already starting to get a moustache. I confirmed that our tickets were good to get in all day long, then we went back outside. I put the receipt and our tickets in my backpack to prove that we had been there, although I felt a little like the super smart criminals who set up their alibis before committing a murder.

Our plan was this: We were going to go to Ladner and hit the comic book store until 1:00 p.m. at the latest. Then we would take the bus and the train back here, giving us a full hour to see the spy exhibit in case our parents asked about it after. No problem.

We walked over to the SkyTrain, and I bought the two tickets from the machine. I could tell that Ali was pretty nervous about it, but I told him it was fine a billion times, and by the time we had to transfer trains, he was chatting away about what comics he was going to look for. I pretended to listen, but in my head I was running through what I was going to say to Auntie Eyeliner.

The ride to Ladner was pretty easy. Two trains, and a transfer to the bus at Bridgeport Station. The bus arrived right on time, and we were at the Ladner bus loop by 11:25. We sat outside the McDonald's and ate two of the samosas that Ali's mom had packed, and we each had an apple from my mom, then walked down Ladner Trunk Road into downtown Ladner.

I had looked at the online maps at least a hundred times, but I was shocked to see that it was way different than Street View showed. For one, the walk in took longer than I thought it would. Then the comic book store was on the left-hand side of the street, but Auntie Eyeliner's garage wasn't in the plaza like I thought, so I figured it was behind it. Except that there was a huge parking lot between them. The two places couldn't be farther apart.

Ali pointed to the comic book store. "It's right there! Let's go!" He took off at a quick pace, heading right. I debated my best option, but I ended up following him.

The store was empty except for a couple of guys

in the back flipping silently through stacks of comics. Ali went straight up to the guy at the counter and started asking questions about Batman back issues. He was right into it. I wandered around the store, flipping aimlessly through a few piles, then I went to the counter.

"I've gotta go to the bathroom," I said to Ali.

"Where are you going to do that?" he asked, looking around the tiny store.

"Subway? Or maybe Safeway?" I said. "I'll find somewhere. I'll be back soon."

I waved as I walked out the door and sauntered out of view of the store. I knew exactly where I was headed, but I didn't want Ali to come find me in the middle of my search.

Now it was time for the real plan to start.

CHAPTER 18

I walked as fast as I could without running across the parking lot. I had to go all the way around the plaza before I could see the Double R Rentals that Auntie Eyeliner owned. It was one of the more run-down buildings around the back. One side was an office, and the other side was a garage and storage space for construction equipment. I didn't want to seem sweaty and nervous, so I took a couple of moments outside to get ready. I pulled the forged letter and the keys out of the front of my backpack. Then, with a deep breath, I entered the office.

I expected it to be full and loud but it was silent except for the buzzer on the door announcing my presence. There wasn't even anyone behind the giant counter that spanned most of the office. The whole place was empty.

I stood there awkwardly until a giant bearded man walked out from the backroom behind the desk, looking bored and angry. "Yes?" he said, already unimpressed.

"Hi, um, I'm here to see Aun— um . . . Elena Arcano," I stammered. It was only at this moment that I realized she might not even work on Saturdays.

The man behind the counter looked down at me, and I stepped back. He was really tall. Like, maybe the size of the Hulk. He opened the door behind him and yelled, "EL!"

Auntie Eyeliner came out of the backroom. When she saw me, she clapped her hands and cried out, "Cooper! What on earth are you doing here? Aw, come here, little guy! Raffi! This is my nephew! Isn't he the handsomest?" She rushed around the counter and hugged me, enveloping me in a fruity perfume. Raffi the Hulk watched for a moment, then went back into the office.

"Auntie Elena, I wanted to see you!" I smiled back, widely. I knew I had to be as charming as possible but also give off a sense of being mature and responsible. I had to be the D.B. Cooper I created, a D.B. Cooper people noticed and paid attention to. D.B. Cooper got what he wanted. I remembered the birthday card I made. "Happy birthday!"

She took the envelope and opened it. "Cooper, my birthday isn't for another two months."

"I know," I said. "But it's got an invitation in it to come to dinner for your birthday."

"I don't see one," she said, looking in the card and the envelope.

"Oh, shoot. I forgot to put it in. It's supposed to be there. I hope you will come!"

I would have to figure out later how to cover this one up with my mom.

"That is so sweet. You are adorable. Of course I will come, I just have to check my schedule. I'm planning on going to Vegas with some girlfriends that weekend, but I can call your mom and plan another day."

I was getting in deeper than I meant to. "Oh, that's okay. I'll get Dad to call you. He's in charge of meals these days. Anyway, um, also, I was kind of hoping you could help me. I need access to Grandpa Cooke's stuff. He has information that I need for my genealogy project at school and Mom said you had his stuff here."

"Oh, I don't know, Cooper. It's all in the back of the garage. It's kind of a pain to get to."

"But he said it was okay. I have the keys here." I smiled at her again, trying to be comforting. "It's a really important project. I have a letter from my teacher if you want to see it."

"Where's your mom? Is she outside?" Auntie Eyeliner asked, scanning the parking lot for my mom's car.

"Oh," I lowered my voice. "She's with Grandpa. He can't leave the hospital." My voice tapered off at the end, and I made sure to look as sad about it as possible. "I'm sure you've heard about it from Dad. He and Mom are really struggling." I said it to make her feel guilty, but as it came out of my mouth I realized how true it really was.

"Right, right. Of course. I keep meaning to call your dad for a catch-up, but you know, life. Hold on, let me see what I can do." Auntie Eyeliner put her hand on my shoulder briefly, then walked away.

The few moments that passed were filled with the echoing silence of the room. All I could hear was my own breathing and the hum of the lights. It felt like eternity. I looked at the clock. I had been gone for five minutes. I figured I had at least fifteen minutes before Ali realized I was still gone and another five while he waited for me to return, but still. I needed into that filing cabinet now. I willed Auntie Eyeliner to move faster.

"All right, Cooper. Come on. Raffi is clearing us a path to your grandfather's stuff. Do you know when your parents are going to come get it? We are getting a new excavator in next month, and I'd love to put it where your grandfather's stuff is."

"I'll let them know. Thanks. This is definitely going to get me an A plus!" I said. I was in! I was going to find out what was in Grandpa's secret cabinet!

Auntie Eyeliner led me through a maze of construction equipment and shelving. At the end of it was Raffi, who was hauling a piece of metal machinery out of the way. He gave me a stink-eye, sweating and breathing heavily, as he passed us.

"Your grandfather's stuff is all right there," Auntie Eyeliner said, pointing to a tightly packed corner of heavy-duty plastic containers.

I could feel something big was going to be there.

I just didn't know where to start. I wandered closer. The boxes were stacked three high, and I could barely reach the lid of the top one. I peered around. I could see the side of the filing cabinet.

Auntie Eyeliner lifted the lid on the top box. "This one is just clothes, it looks like." She hefted it off the top and moved it aside. I opened it up too, just in case what she thought were clothes were actually D.B. Cooper's used parachutes. But unless his parachutes were green-and-blue plaid, they were definitely clothes. Meanwhile, Auntie Eyeliner opened the next box. "This one too." She opened the last box. "Also clothes."

"You don't have to stay here," I said, after she had moved all the boxes out of the way of the filing cabinet. "I'll be okay by myself."

She stood up and wiped her hands on her pants. "Sure, if you don't mind. I've got a few things to take care of in the office. I'll get Raffi to keep the door open, so yell for him if you need anything." I knew I would not be needing anything from Raffi, but I smiled and thanked her anyway.

Once she was gone I pulled the keys out of my pocket. I took a moment then to mark what was about to happen. I was about to crack this case wide open. After that, I put the key in the filing cabinet.

It didn't work. I tried to turn it, but nothing. How could a key fit in a lock but not actually do anything?

Luckily I had two keys. I put in the other one,

which was stickier and I had to kind of jam it in, but I got it there. Then I tried to turn it. Again, nothing. Except that didn't make sense. The keys had to be for the filing cabinet. I yanked hard on the key. Harder. Then, just as I was about to lose it, the key turned. I had all my weight on the key, so when it moved I stumbled backwards. I grabbed on to the filing cabinet as I started to fall and tripped back, bringing the filing cabinet with me. Luckily the other boxes were right behind me, so I didn't fall all the way back, just on an angle that made it awkward to get up. I tried pushing the filing cabinet up, but it was too heavy. I was stuck.

"Uh, Raffi? Raffi?" I called out. My voice echoed in the cold concrete room. I heard his thudding footsteps come closer. His frame blocked out the light, and he laughed when he saw what had happened. His laugh was big and loud. Without saying anything but still chuckling, Raffi pulled the filing cabinet back to upright, then pulled me up by the arm.

"Good?" he asked. I nodded, rubbing my arm where I'd gotten pinned. I was sure that was going to leave a bruise.

After he left I was careful when opening the drawers. There were only two with stuff in them. The top drawer was all old bank and tax statements, filed and identified by year, going back to 1972. The bottom drawer, though, was suspiciously empty except for a few things.

I decided the best way to attack the drawer was

to take everything out. I lined up the three bins of clothes as a makeshift table, then started going through it. I pulled out my notebook and got to work, noting anything that was of interest.

CASE: 0024 / FILE: 0006
LOCATION: Ladner, British Columbia

A File on "Alleged" D.B. Cooper's Files

From 2007: Agent Cooper Arcano birth announcement

Wedding photo of Agents Marco Arcano and Dawn Cooke-Arcano at the church

Photo of Aunt Jane and Uncle Bryan at their cottage in Ontario

Three dated and identified photos: 1978 — Dawn Cooke (baby picture); 1980 — Jane Cooke (baby picture); 1996 — Dawn Cooke with Jane Cooke (Dawn's high-school graduation)

Envelope containing mortgage papers from 1986 for house in Ladner

Box containing two wedding rings, one men's, one women's. Diamond is clearly missing from the setting (possibly used as collateral??)

More photos of random people unidentified on back (4 of them)

An ugly velvet jewellery box, like, seriously ugly. Blue velvet on the bottom, strange pink and green flowers on the top. Inside the box are three sparkly necklaces. They don't look like diamonds, but they are very sparkly. (Agent Cooper jokes to himself, "I don't imagine D.B. Cooper wore them often, maybe only for special occasions.")

A set of dog tags. One side had the seal of the US Navy, and the other side read:

COOKE

BARTHOLOMEW D

198-946-998

A POS

CHRISTIAN

More photos of unidentified people, including one of ~~Grandpa~~ alleged D.B. Cooper in his uniform, standing with three other men who are not in uniform.

Deed for house in Tsawwassen in 1975

END MISSIVE

There were a few things in there that could be useful. The photos of people I didn't know: one set of them was obviously really old. The people were dressed like hippies in three of them, and two of them were black and white. These could be important, maybe like accomplices along the way.

By far, the most interesting thing was the dog tags. I held them up to look at them closely. They looked real, although I had never seen dog tags before. Bartholomew D. Cooke? The "D" could stand for anything, like Dan . . . or Don. Bartholomew DON Cooke? B.D. Cooke? That sounded a lot like

D.B. Cooper. Especially if you were in a rush to come up with an alias. Not only that, but my blood type was A-positive as well, and I'm pretty sure blood type runs in the family. So it all lined up. These dog tags were my link to D.B. Cooper. Except for the exact name, but of course Grandpa wouldn't have used his real name if he was hijacking a plane. Then he probably dropped the Bartholomew part when he got to Canada to keep the FBI off his trail. That's what I would do, and we clearly thought the same way, being related and all.

I laughed out loud. I had practically solved it! I knew it was worth coming to Ladner! I thought about taking the dog tags but I knew that would be a bad idea. Plus, I had the information — I didn't need the actual dog tags. I quickly put everything back in the bottom drawer, although I took the photos and put them in my backpack just in case. No one would miss them, I was sure. Then I went to find Auntie Eyeliner in her office.

"Did you find what you need?" she asked.

I smiled as confidently as D.B. Cooper probably did to the flight attendant in 1971. "I sure did. You're the best aunt ever. I'll make sure to write that in my report too."

I looked over at the wall clock. It was already 12:40! I'd been there for forty-five minutes! I thanked Auntie Eyeliner again and told her that I would get Dad to call and invite her for dinner, and then I ran out the door.

CHAPTER 19

I looked out for cars and darted back across the parking lot. I sprinted to the comic book store. I pulled open the door and looked around. Ali wasn't there.

"Did you see my friend?" I asked the cashier. He shook his head.

"Nope." The guy didn't even look up at me.

"He was here before. He came to get his Batman valued. You guys talked about it. He's tall? Dark brown hair? Kind of has a moustache? You guys were talking about Batman." I described Ali as best I could. The guy shook his head again.

"I know who you mean. Cool kid. He left a little while ago." He looked up. "I think he went to find you."

"Where did he go to find me?" I asked, a little in shock that someone referred to Ali as being cool. Ali and I aren't cool at all. We know that.

"Dunno. Out there." the guy gestured vaguely behind him at the parking lot.

"Great," I mumbled. I didn't know what to do. We only had Ali's mom's phone with us, and I didn't have the number. I went outside and hung around in front of the shop for another five minutes, scanning for Ali. No sign of him.

Okay. I was panicking. Where did Ali go to look for me? Why didn't he come back here? We both knew the plan was to catch the 1:25 bus back to the SkyTrain. The way I saw it, I had two options: I could wait here and see if Ali returned to the comic book store or I could walk back to the bus loop to wait for him there. Either way, I had to get back to Vancouver. Neither option was particularly good. I wished that Ali would just appear in front of me, so I closed my eyes and imagined him there. I opened my eyes, hoping he would be walking across the parking lot, but there was only an elderly couple shuffling their way to the ABC restaurant. I waited outside the store for an excruciating fifteen minutes, but he never showed. I went back into the store.

"Hey," I said to the cashier. "Hey. If my friend Ali comes back in here looking for me, can you tell him that I went to find him at the bus loop?"

The cashier nodded absentmindedly. "Yup."

"So you'll tell my friend Ali that I went to find him at the Ladner bus loop? I'll be at the Ladner bus loop," I repeated.

"Yup," the cashier said.

"Okay. Thanks. I'm off to the Ladner bus loop now," I said again for good measure.

"Yup," the cashier said.

I left and looked around the parking lot one more time. No Ali, so I walked back to the bus loop. The whole walk back, I was running through worst-case scenarios. Like what if he called my parents because he couldn't find me? Or if he called his parents? Or what if he got lost on the bus on the way home alone and ended up in Seattle?

Or what if Ali got kidnapped while he was looking for me? He was so trusting of people that he could easily have asked the wrong people about me, and then gotten into a windowless van with a bunch of gangsters and now be in trouble. Or maybe he panicked, ran out into the parking lot without looking, and got run over by the elderly couple going to the ABC restaurant. They had adrenalin-fuelled superhuman strength and just put Ali's body in their trunk before heading for pancakes!

There were so many scenarios, and I played them all out in my head as I speed-walked to the bus stop.

As I turned the corner I saw my bus pulling out. "Hey!!! Hey! STOP!!" I jumped up and down, waving my arms like a crazy person. But the driver didn't stop. She turned right onto Ladner Trunk Road, leaving me behind. And as I watched the bus speed up and pull away, I caught a glimpse of Ali looking out the back window, holding a cellphone to his ear.

I had half an hour to kill before the next bus to

Bridgeport Station, so I sat at the playground by the bus stop and stewed. I thought about how worried I was that Ali was dead, but now that I knew he had abandoned me in Ladner, I felt like I wanted some of those things to happen to him.

I imagined all the things that happened to television Dana Scully when she was separated from Fox Mulder on *The X-Files*. She almost froze to death, she was abducted by aliens, she was kidnapped several times . . . Any of these things would be better than seeing Ali abandon me while he was probably calling my parents to tell on me. I couldn't believe I was worried about that guy! I also realized while sitting there that Ali had all the good snacks in his bag, and all I had was two apples. I ate one of them while imagining Ali's alien abduction. Finally the bus arrived and I jumped on.

It felt like forever before we got to Bridgeport Station and I tried to pass the time thinking of how I was going to confirm that Bartholomew D. Cooke was connected to Grandpa and D.B. Cooper. It was too close; these names had to all fit together somehow.

Once the bus arrived at the SkyTrain station, I looked everywhere for Ali. It felt strange being alone. I was sure everyone was watching me, wondering why a kid was alone. One woman even asked if I was lost. I figured Ali had enough sense to wait for me at Bridgeport Station, but he was nowhere to be found. I wished I had a cellphone so that I could text him to tell him we were no longer friends. What was he doing to me?

I got on the next train and looked for him at Waterfront Station. Again, no luck. There were more people here, and some of them looked a bit scary. It also smelled a lot like pee. I avoided a guy and girl who were sitting on the floor with a giant dog and hurried to the other platform. Here it felt like no one was watching me, and that was even creepier than at Bridgeport. I guess he thought he should just meet me at Science World, which was really dumb, but at least I knew he was on his way.

I caught the next train and got off at Main Street–Science World Station, sure I would see Ali waiting there for me. He wasn't. I wanted to yell at him so badly that I stormed out of the station and ran across the street toward Science World. Once I was at street level I saw Ali. He was standing in front of Science World, but not right outside, closer to the street than the entrance. I waited on the other side of the intersection for the light to change, and then I ran over to him, already yelling.

"Why didn't you wait for me?!" I said, at the same time that he was yelling back at me, "Where did you go?!"

I got to the other side of the street, trying to explain what happened, alternating with questions about why he was such a dummy, but Ali stopped me in mid-yell when he said, "Your dad is coming here."

"You called my dad?!"

"I couldn't find you, Cooper! I couldn't find you and I waited and I waited and I didn't know what to do because my mom would kill me if we were in Ladner, and I needed help finding you, so I called your house just to see if you called there and then I had to lie to your dad and say that I just lost track of you at Science World and he said he was coming down here. I tried to tell him not to, and then I even called back when I saw you running for the bus. But he said that he was coming here early to get us because we weren't acting maturely!" Ali was breathless and almost in tears.

I was still angry, but I also felt pretty terrible for putting Ali in this position. I didn't know what to do. Ali swore under his breath, and I looked around.

"Well, um, let's go in," I said. "We can pretend we were in the IMAX movie. I'll say I saw it twice and that's why we got separated, because . . . because I went to the washroom and I thought you said that you were going to the movie so I went to the movie and then it started and I'd already paid for it, and I just figured you were sitting on the other side of the theatre."

My plan was falling into place. "So then you couldn't find me because you hadn't gone to the movie so you called home, but then you did find me and you were mad at me for seeing the movie, right? And you made me go see it again . . . And, oh yeah, your cell was turned off because it was a movie!" Ali was nodding in agreement.

"Yeah, yeah. That works," he said. We started walking toward the entrance. "When did you get so good at lying?" he asked. "And where did you go?"

"I went to the bank," I said. "I thought they would have the nicest bathroom."

Ali looked like he wanted to say something about how long I was gone, but then he decided not to. He nodded again and didn't ask any more questions.

Which was good, because standing inside the entrance to Science World was my father. And he was not happy.

CHAPTER 20

CASE: 0024 / FILE: 0007
LOCATION: Vancouver, British Columbia

The following is a transcript of the disciplinary hearing for Agent Cooper Arcano. Note that the transcript has been redacted for inappropriate language use.

AGENT MARCO: Where the ██████ have you been?

AGENT COOPER: Here. We just went outside to have lunch.

AGENT ALI: We were here the whole time. We were just eating lunch outside. We had White Spot burgers and mine had a side of fries, but Cooper got a side of sweet potato fries. This was because we went to the IMAX movie over lunch, and — Ow! That's what we did. That's all we did.

AGENT MARCO: Ali Singh, you called and told me Cooper was missing. Missing, you said. (To staff) Thanks for your help, and sorry. Sorry. (To agents) Get in the car, boys. We'll talk about this on the way home.

AGENT COOPER: Dad, you didn't have to come early. We just misplaced each other. It's not a big deal.

AGENT MARCO: It IS a big deal. It's a ▆▆▆▆▆▆▆ big deal, Cooper! We trusted you; we trusted you and Ali to act like mature teenagers, and then you lose each other? In a metallic bubble? You know better!

AGENT COOPER: Nothing happened, Dad!

AGENT MARCO: Nothing happened? Then why did you two come sauntering inside while I'm in there like a fool getting the whole staff to look for you? You know they were going to put the place on lockdown for you fools? They were this close to lockdown! You don't leave each other's side! You don't call home saying you're missing! You're very lucky it was me coming down here, and not your mother! And Ali! Your mother was already worried about you coming here and then you go and break our trust? You two should be grounded for life!

AGENT COOPER: We're really sorry, Dad. See, what happened was . . .

AGENT MARCO: I don't need or want your explanation, Cooper. I don't know what story you've cooked up, but I don't want to hear it.

AGENT ALI: Are you going to tell my mom? We're really sorry.

AGENT MARCO: Not as sorry as you'll be when you're still grounded three years from now.

END MISSIVE

Ali lucked out; only his sister, Surya, was home when we dropped him off, so there was no parent for my dad to talk to. Ali was clearly panicking since he had started crying when my dad was yelling at us, but I knew that Dad would calm down and things would blow over. After all, it wasn't that bad, was it? He didn't know we went to Ladner. I could change our story to say that we went to get ice cream up the street and the line was long. At least I had the information I needed for my case and Ali didn't get in trouble, plus I bet he bought a few comics too. I doubted he was so worried that he didn't buy a couple of things.

What I didn't know was that Dad had told Mom where he was going. I thought maybe we had a father-son understanding that Mom didn't need to know about Ali and me disappearing from Science World. And this meant that I wasn't ready for the firestorm of anger when I walked in the door. Suffice to say, I was grounded. Grounded for a long time, and I probably won't get to go to Science World again until I'm nineteen.

I spent the rest of Saturday in my room, locked away from the remaining wrath of my parents as they wore themselves out being angry. At first they were both angry with me, then the fight turned and they were angry with each other about me being missing, then they were angry with each other about something totally unrelated, and then I heard the door to the garage slam, followed by silence.

I heard the phone ring once, and I could tell it was Ali on the other end, but then I heard my mother ask to speak to Mrs. Singh. I listened in to the conversation, and it didn't sound good. I knew it was all over for him too.

The only upside was that I had something. I knew about Bartholomew D. Cooke, and I had new photos to add to my files. After lying on my bed doing nothing for a long while I got up and put the photos inside my nightstand drawer. I also put the keys back in there, and I ripped up the fake letter I had concocted. I knew that Scully would have never let Mulder shred evidence, but I also knew that if my evidence got into the wrong hands, things could get worse.

***

The only thing I was allowed to do on Sunday was visit Grandpa, which worked out in my favour. For one thing, I had to put the keys back before Grandpa noticed they were gone. I needed a reason for us to be in his room. I got a few photos from the storage box downstairs and brought them up, adding the filing-cabinet photos to the pile.

"I thought we could take some photos for Grandpa this week," I said, showing my mom the stack of photos. "Maybe he'll like that. They'll be different than the ones at his place."

Mom dried her hands from washing the dishes and looked at me. "You don't need to suck up, you know. You're still going to be grounded."

"Yeah, I know. I'm really sorry for yesterday. We shouldn't have gone for ice cream, but I still don't think it was a big deal." *Especially considering where we really went*, I thought, but I bit my tongue. And I *was* sorry. I didn't like that we got caught and that I had made things even worse at home. I could tell she was getting ready to launch into another speech, so I quickly kept talking. "I mean, I get it. I do. I know we shouldn't have left Science World. I'm sorry, Mom. The photos are just so that today's not boring. I'm trying to be helpful."

Mom relented a little. "Fine. Bring them. Get ready. We're leaving in fifteen minutes." I knew it would be a few more days before Mom was back to being nice Mom. I was also pretty sure that any minute now my parents were going to announce their divorce, so I had to move quickly. Until then, I had to be the nicest version of myself I could be so that maybe they would hold off until I could prove my theory.

I ran upstairs and rescued the keys from my nightstand, then grabbed a hoodie from the pile in front of the closet. Dana Scully looked really excited and started jumping up on my pant leg like we were going to go for a walk.

"Later, Scully. I've got work to do first," I told her. I don't think she understood.

I pulled my sneakers on. "Ready when you are!" I called.

The ride was all radio, no discussion. I wanted

to say something, but I didn't know what would be the best topic of conversation since, in just one day, my mom had developed this amazing ability to turn anything into a lecture about being mature and responsible. So I just kept my mouth shut.

We got to Golden Sunsets in record time. It was one of those nice fall days where the sun still has some heat to it. I saw that Mrs. Kim was sitting outside on a bench with a few of the other old people and one of the nurses. I jogged over while Mom got her things together.

She smiled when she saw me.

"Hello!" she said brightly.

"Hi, Mrs. Kim," I said. "How are you today?"

"Oh, you came to say hello to me! I thought you knew one of these other fine people. You'll have to forgive me, I don't remember who you are. I have a touch of the Alzheimer's," she said.

"Yeah, I know. You told me before," I said.

She frowned. "I did? I'm so sorry! I'm so stupid," she chastised herself, shaking her head slowly.

"It's okay," I said. "I don't mind."

She frowned. "No, it's not okay. Stupid, stupid Yireh." She looked close to tears.

Mom had caught up and gave me an accusing look. "Cooper, let's go in. She doesn't want to be bothered."

"I'm not bothering her, Mom. I was just saying hello." I couldn't win this weekend.

Mrs. Kim's tears had started to spill over, and

the nurse had come over to comfort her. She was still mumbling "stupid, stupid, stupid" as we walked inside.

I felt terrible. I wanted to tell her about how I'd made a breakthrough in our unsolved mystery. She would have been so excited to hear about it, even if she didn't really remember what the case was.

I followed Mom in, looking back at Mrs. Kim sitting in the sunshine, weeping.

Grandpa was no better. He was in his room when we got there, and he was surrounded by all the clothes from his closet. They were strewn across the floor but Grandpa was still in his dressing gown. He was sitting on the bed, staring out the window.

"Dad? It's Dawn, your daughter," Mom said, standing tentatively at the door.

"No, no," he said, looking at Mom briefly but then going back to the window.

"It's me. I'm here with your grandson, Cooper. We came to visit," she said.

"No, no," he mumbled again, but we entered the room anyway. Mom picked up some of the clothes on the floor. "What have you been doing here, Dad? Were you looking for something in particular?"

I gulped. What if he had been looking for the keys and I caused this? I started picking up clothes too.

"In here?" I asked, opening the top drawer and throwing the clothes on top of the socks and underwear. "Nope. Not in here," I said, grabbing the keys from my pocket and shoving my hand under the clothes. I felt around blindly, which caused me to touch some of Grandpa's underwear. I wanted to make noise about it, but I swallowed back my disgust for the sake of the mission and found a pair of socks. I tucked the keys into the socks and grabbed the clothes out of the drawer.

Grandpa was basically ignoring us, so Mom and I hung all his clothes back in the closet.

"Linda?" Grandpa said.

Mom blanched. "No, Dad. It's me, Dawn. Linda was your wife. I'm your daughter."

"No, Linda. No," he said. I turned around. He was looking at Mom, but he was shaking his head. "No, no. Dawn is—" He mimed holding a baby.

"Dad, I'm Dawn. I grew up!" she said, with fake enthusiasm. She gestured to me and whispered, "Where are the photos you brought?"

I patted down my pockets, but I couldn't find them.

"I think I left them on my bed," I whispered back. "I'm sorry. I meant to bring them." I didn't like seeing Grandpa like this. It was creepier than when he yelled at me about the broken lamp, and it scared me.

Mom must have sensed something. "It's fine," she said gently.

She handed the last two shirts in her arms to me and crossed the room. "Here, Dad. I'll show you," she said.

Grandpa watched her suspiciously from his perch on the bed.

"Linda, where's—" then he paused.

"Dawn!" he called.

"Dad, I'm right here. I'm Dawn." She leaned down to pull out one of the photo albums on the bookshelf.

"Linda, you can't leave the baby alone upstairs," he said, chastising my mom. I looked at her. What was he talking about?

Mom was flipping through the pages to find a good photo. "He's just confused. He's mixed up me and Grandma," she whispered. "See, Dad? Here's all of us at Mom's birthday when I was thirteen. My mom is Linda. She's the one in the centre. I'm Dawn. I'm the kid in white. Your other daughter, Jane, is wearing the firefighter's hat. Here, this is me on the side, holding the cake." She pointed at the page she had chosen. Grandpa kept shaking his head. She pointed to the next page. "And here's me at my high-school grad. You and Mom came. This is the only photo from that day because you forgot to bring a second roll of film and you refused to get a digital camera because they were pretty new back then." She flipped back a few pages. "See? This is me as a baby, but I grew up."

Mom's voice sounded like she was trying to be calm, but I could tell she was getting a little panicky too.

"No!" Grandpa hit the photo album out of Mom's

hand, and it landed face down on the floor, the pages bent in different directions under the weight of the cover.

Mom backed away. I could tell she was upset, but I didn't know what to do about it.

"Mom? I . . . um . . . I forgot that I have a math test tomorrow. Can we go home soon?" I said cautiously.

Mom was still looking at the album on the floor. "Yeah, sure, honey. You should study." She breathed deeply in and out a few breaths, then she spoke in a clear voice. "Dad, we've got to go, okay? Cooper has a test to study for, and I've got to get dinner ready. But we love you, okay?"

I didn't say anything. Mom's hand was heavy on my shoulder. Grandpa returned to staring out the window, like we'd never entered the room. We left the photo album on the floor and went home.

CHAPTER 21

The silence coming home was different than the one going to see Grandpa. I struggled to find something to say to Mom. Every time I looked over at her she looked like she was going to start crying but it was like she was trying to hide it from me, so I didn't want to make a big deal about it.

Finally Mom said, "He hasn't said my name in months." I didn't think she was saying it to me, but I felt like I was supposed to respond.

"Oh." I struggled for something to say. "Maybe he didn't recognize you because your hair was so big in your grad photo. It was, like, a foot in the air."

Mom coughed and laughed at the same time. "The nineties were not a good fashion time."

"That's an understatement," I said.

We both went silent again for the rest of the way. Mom feeling bad made me angry at Grandpa. We drove all the way out to see him every single week. Mom always tried her best, and then he has to be a jerk to her? Plus I was almost certain he was faking, so wasn't this taking things too far? How far would D.B. Cooper go to protect his identity? I wasn't sure I wanted to find out. But if he was going to care only about himself, then I was too. If he wasn't going to tell us his real secret, then maybe it was time to go in a different direction with my case.

At home, Mom poured herself a glass of wine and curled into her chair in the family room. I grabbed the leash and took Dana Scully out for a walk.

I walked for a long time, planning my next move on the case. As far as I saw, I had three options. Option one: Prove to Tristan that my grandfather was D.B. Cooper so that I could get two hundred dollars. I didn't have a lot of time left in our bet, three weeks max.

Second option: Prove to Mom and Dad that Grandpa was D.B. Cooper and tell them about the money. Then we could decide together what to do about it. We could have a meeting with Grandpa and tell him that we knew; we could sneak him out and put him somewhere he wouldn't be discovered. I pictured myself receiving postcards from different locations around the world, all signed "Love, D.B.C." I would know he was safe and getting to see Cuba or wherever he wanted to go. It was a pretty happy ending.

The last option was to not tell Mom, Dad or Grandpa that I knew his secret, and turn him in to the FBI to get the reward money for finding D.B.

Cooper. I would get invited to be on talk shows and the news; maybe I would write a book about my hunt? Or maybe a comic book or graphic novel; writing a book sounded like a lot of work. But I could make way more than $100,000. Plus I could take Ali with me when I went to New York and LA and places, which would be way better than leaving him at home to be friends with Tristan. Handing Grandpa over to the Feds was the best idea. I felt guilty that I was going to have to betray Grandpa, but wasn't it better to keep my parents together? It looked like the only way to solve everyone's problems.

So what was missing? What was the final piece to prove that Grandpa was D.B. Cooper? I thought about it for my whole walk, but I just couldn't come up with anything.

***

Monday at school, Ali ignored me. I tried to get his attention but any time I caught his eye he looked away. He avoided me at recess by playing soccer, leaving me to basically kick dirt around the playground by myself. I finally was able to corner him when he was coming out of the bathroom and my class was on the way to our library period.

"Ali, I'm sorry about Saturday," I whispered.

"Do you know how much trouble I'm in? My parents are never going to let me have any friends again," he hissed.

"Me neither. But you're the one who left me behind!" I countered.

"You disappeared!!"

I smiled a little, thinking about how similar I was to D.B. Cooper with my ability to disappear.

"What? Do you think it's funny?! You think you're so smart! Dude, you are so . . . argh!!" Ali walked away, leaving me alone in the hall.

I felt awful. I didn't know what to do to make him less mad at me. I wished I had money to buy him something, but I wasn't sure that would even help. With him and my parents being angry, I felt totally alone. I went into the library and sat down between the bookshelves, hidden away so I could feel bad for myself in peace.

Grounded and friendless, I worked on my crime board, especially since Mom and Dad had cut off my screen time, and I was only allowed the computer for half an hour of "homework time." They had tried this restriction before but never actually stuck to it, so I was surprised that Mom set a timer each time I turned on the computer. They were serious this time, and it sucked. How was I going to learn anything about Bartholomew D. Cooke without the internet? I begged for more time to work on my "school project," but Mom said that if I was that intent on getting one hundred percent, I should use my lunch break to do work in the library.

I tried to call Ali a few times in the evenings, but either he really wasn't allowed to talk on the phone or he was full-on avoiding me. It might have been both. As I watched him out on the soccer field at recess, I thought that maybe he really wasn't going to be my friend anymore.

Tristan still said hi to me, but I tried to ignore him. It felt like he was just rubbing it in that he was going to be Ali's best friend.

So I did what Mom suggested. I spent my lunch hours in the library. Not that it mattered all that much. My internet searches didn't bring up anything linking D.B. Cooper and B.D. Cooke, or anything on B.D. Cooke at all. Eventually I realized that it was better to go straight to the source anyway. Maybe me saying the name Bartholomew D. Cooke would let Grandpa know I was in on his secret, and I could get to the heart of this mystery. I mean, it had to have been him, right? The same initials were too much of a coincidence not to be.

This meant I had to plan an interrogation. I wondered if Golden Sunsets had an empty room with just a table, two chairs and a bright light, but I doubted it. But it was okay: if I was anything like Fox Mulder, I could succeed with minimal resources.

CHAPTER 22

By Thursday I had planned out exactly how my interrogation would go. Even someone with Alzheimer's would crack under the pressure I was going to apply. Because Dana Scully is just a dog, I knew that I would have to play good cop AND bad cop. Also, with Mom probably being in the room I would have to be sneaky about my questioning. Since I'd already gotten in trouble for bringing up D.B. Cooper before, I wrote out questions that only the real D.B. Cooper would know the answers to.

CASE: 0024 / FILE: 0008
LOCATION: Vancouver, British Columbia
Interrogation Practice by Agent Cooper Arcano

(Note: These are written in a specific order!!!) Hey, what's this in my backpack? (pulls out composite drawing of D.B. Cooper) It looks like my art project from this week. We were drawing people. Does this guy look familiar to you, Grandpa?

Hey, he looks a lot like you, Grandpa. Do you think

I actually drew a picture from memory of you when you were younger?

Ha! You think it's you, but I didn't draw you! It's actually someone really famous! Do you know who it is?

Maybe you've heard the name Bartholomew before? Have you heard that name?

Ha! Care to tell us any more about this "Bartholomew D. Cooke"?

Would you be able to pick him out of a lineup?

We know you can't leave Golden Sunsets. Lucky for you we've brought the lineup to you! Look at this photo! (pulls out photo taken from filing cabinet)

Which one of these men is Bartholomew D. Cooke?

Where did I get this photo, you ask? A good agent has ways and means . . .

Oh, the one in the middle. Why, Grandpa, that's you. YOU'RE Bartholomew D. Cooke? Well, now, isn't that interesting . . .

Do you know what your blood type is?

Where were you on November 24, 1971?

You can't remember? You can't . . . REMEM-BER?!?! I'm surprised. I would think that you would always remember November 24, 1971.

Now, Grandpa, calm down. We're just having a little chat. That's all. You like chats, right? You remember having little chats?

So, what if I show you this drawing and say

"November 24, 1971"? Are you getting it yet, Grandpa?? Or should I say . . . D.B. COOPER????

END MISSIVE

All of my planning was for nothing. The phone rang on Thursday evening, and the call display showed that it was Golden Sunsets. When Mom got off the phone, she turned to me.

"Well, you're going to be happy," she said.

"Am I allowed to bring Dana Scully this week?"

"We aren't going at all. There's been a few cases of the flu, so the whole facility is on quarantine lockdown. They've asked that there be no visitors until it's passed," Mom said, and then looked at my dad. "You're on deck now, Mr. Arcano. You have to entertain both of us all day on Sunday."

I groaned. "Are you sure? Can't we go anyway?"

Dad looked at me like I was crazy. "Why do you want to go? We can do something fun instead of visiting the old folks! We could fly off to Vegas! Make a million dollars at blackjack!"

"It's just that . . . I have a genealogy project at school. I wanted to look at Grandpa's photo albums to get some better pictures. I need to know a bunch about my family, and it's due next week," I lied.

"Cooper, haven't you been working on that for a month? You've had plenty of visits to get photos. Why did you leave it until the last minute?" Mom said.

"I don't know," I muttered. I had forgotten that I used it as an excuse a while ago.

"Well, I guess we can work on that together on Sunday," Dad said. "I'm off the hook! And to think I was going to take you both to Vegas for the weekend. Too bad about that genealogy project getting in the way."

"We can't afford Vegas," Mom said, staring at Dad.

"Relax, Dawn. It was a joke." He stared right back at her.

She ignored him and turned to me. "Why don't you go get it and do it right now?"

"Never mind, guys. It's not really that big. I left it at school. There isn't really a due date." I tried to backpedal.

"Cooper, don't leave things to the last minute. Bring it home tomorrow and we can sit down and go through it together," Mom said sternly.

"Yeah, fine," I said. "I'll bring it home. Can I use the computer? I want to start working on my story for English class."

I got permission for extra screen time and holed myself up with Dana Scully. Then I frantically made myself a worksheet that I could "bring home." It had a bunch of questions that I could fill in about my grandparents and parents, and I figured it would work as my fake project. I stopped a few times while I was working to look at the photos on the family wall. I sighed. How did I end up making up fake homework instead of solving an unsolved mystery?

My Friday-night fake homework session started after supper. I thought I would get out of it, and that my mom would have forgotten, but as soon as supper was over she poured herself and my dad each a glass of wine.

"Let's see this genealogy project," she said, settling in at the kitchen table while Dad took the compost out.

I ran upstairs and grabbed the "homework" sheets I printed off the night before.

"Here they are. I already grabbed a bunch of photos from downstairs, so I just need to fill in some information about people." I flattened the sheets on the table.

Mom read them over quickly. "What is this? This is your homework?"

"Yeah. Weird, right?"

"Weird doesn't begin to cover it. What are these questions? This looks like a kid made it. Your teacher came up with them?" She flipped over the pages to see if there was something else on the back.

"Yup. She made them all up. They are so weird, though. That's why it's taking me so long to do the project." I whined a little, trying to gain some sympathy.

"'What was your grandfather's profession?' is a question I understand, but why is 'What is your grandfather's favourite television show?' on here? And 'If your grandfather was a spy, what would his code name be?' Cooper, this is just bizarre."

Dad came in and sat down, picking up the second sheet of paper. "'What is your grandmother's view on committing a crime?' 'What kind of person was your grandfather in 1970?' This is your homework?" Dad laughed.

"Well, we brainstormed questions as a class and these are the best ones we could come up with. It's not that dumb!" I was getting kind of mad with how they were mocking my questions. I spent quite a bit of time coming up with questions that might actually help me with my D.B. Cooper case.

"Are you supposed to just guess at some of this?" Mom asked.

"Well, don't you know? What was your mom like? What was Grandpa before he retired?" I asked.

Dad put down the paper. "We can call my parents in the morning if you want. They'll answer all your weirdo questions. The rest is up to your mom. We'll be watching the game if you need us." He picked up Dana Scully and left us.

So Mom and I sat at the kitchen table and filled in what we could of my questions. And it turned out she knew a lot more about Grandpa than she was letting on.

The biggest news: Grandpa's first name is Bartholomew, but he "goes by" his middle name, which is Donald. So I was right! I didn't even have to interrogate him to confirm it. When Mom told me that I made a mental note to look up the US Navy and see if they had paratroopers.

As she made her way through her glass of wine, she talked more and more about growing up. I never really knew my grandma, but she sounded like she was an awesome kind of crazy. Apparently Grandma loved square dancing and had all the outfits for it. Mom said that it was so embarrassing as a teenager because Grandma would make them all practise the patterns in the living room, and Mom would have to dance with a doll as her partner. I couldn't imagine Grandpa dancing at all, but Mom said that he would grumble about it, but he would always do it.

Mom's first job was at the McDonald's in Ladner, and every morning Grandma and Grandpa would walk there to have a coffee. Mom said it drove her crazy that they would sit and watch her work. Even after she quit they still went every day, and when Grandma got sick they would drive there so that they could keep going.

I learned that Grandma was from Vancouver, which was weird, because Grandpa was from Chicago. I asked Mom how they met, and she said that they were both on vacation in Seaside, Oregon, with their families and fell in love as teenagers. So, they wrote letters and talked on the phone for years before Grandpa could get to Vancouver.

But here's the interesting part: Grandpa moved from Chicago to Washington to be closer to my grandma. Grandpa lived in Everett for a few years, which made sense for why D.B. Cooper would have been in Washington when he hijacked the plane. And falling in love with Grandma, who lived in Canada? This gave him a first-class motive for wanting a ton of money and for jumping out of a plane. I figured there was probably another layer to the story: maybe his parents had wanted him to marry another girl and he defied them to marry Grandma. I asked what Grandpa's parents were like, but Mom said that Grandpa had had a huge fight with his parents when he moved to Everett, and so she never met them. This seemed very suspicious, but it definitely added to the plausibility of my D.B. Cooper theory.

At the end of the night, Mom looked pretty relaxed and almost happy. "That was fun, honey. I should use some of that in my scrapbook," she said.

"Definitely, Mom. Thanks for the intel," I replied, gathering up my notes. She got up and went into the TV room where Dad was sitting. I paused, waiting to hear what came next, but there was no noise. I peeked inside, and Mom was sitting next to Dad on the couch, her feet up in his lap. I smiled and went to bed.

All in all, my fake homework turned out to be very useful indeed.

CHAPTER 23

Now that I knew for sure that Grandpa's initials were the same as D.B. Cooper's, that he HAD been in the navy (which, by the way, does have a parachute unit; I looked it up), and that he lived in Everett (which, by the way, is where the Boeing factory is!) and had a motive for getting a lot of money and running away to Canada (true love seemed like a good reason to me), I was even more disappointed to not see him on Sunday. I had clues! I had information! I had facts! The whole case was about to break wide open, and I was trapped.

Plus, I was still grounded from my trip to "Science World," so I wasn't allowed to do anything other than walk the dog. I worked on my crime board, making sure that all my new information was properly documented, and I updated my interrogation questions multiple times, but I was stalled. It sucked.

I was so lonely not having Ali to talk to that I had to do something to win him back. So, on

Tuesday I ran up to him before class started and pushed my pencil crayons into his chest.

"These are for you," I said.

"What? Why?"

"I know they're not great, but you can keep them until I can afford to get you really good ones for our comic book. And I'll get you fancy pens and ink and the full one hundred pencil crayons in the metal case. I used these a couple times, but they're still okay," I explained. He looked super confused. "They're a sorry present. For ditching you in Ladner."

He handed back the box. "I have pencil crayons."

"I know, but I don't know what else to do. I kind of need you to be my best friend. So, take these and once I win the bet with Tristan I can buy you really good ones," I pleaded with him.

"I am your best friend. Dude. You're being weird," he said.

"Are you sure? Because you haven't talked to me in forever," I said.

He shrugged, kind of embarrassed. "It hasn't been that long. I've just been busy. And grounded. Both."

"But you're not mad?" I asked.

"Not really. I mean, kind of, actually. But not really."

"Oh. Okay." I put the pencil crayons back in my bag and we stood there awkwardly.

"I guess I'll go hang my stuff up," I said.

"'Kay. See ya," Ali replied.

I couldn't tell if my plan had worked or not, but at least I knew Ali would talk to me. I nodded to myself. I would still get him a present when I won. And I would give it to him in front of Tristan.

By Wednesday night all the love that I thought I had created at home over the weekend was gone. Mom and Dad got into a huge fight after I went to bed. It had been tense all evening, starting with an argument about who was going to do the dishes, and then it really got going after I was sent to bed. I lay there listening to Mom's voice get higher in volume and pitch and Dad saying less and less. The fight was about money, that much I knew. Something about Auntie Jane not helping out with Grandpa's care, and Mom not working full-time; I didn't know all the details. I tried to drown it out by playing the Star Wars soundtrack to get to sleep, but the "Imperial March" sure wasn't helping me forget about the impending split of my family. I finally fell asleep, Dana Scully curled in my arms and sharing my pillow, and I dreamt of the destruction of the Death Star, with my grandfather being Darth Vader.

Dad was the one who woke me up the next morning.

"Where's Mom?" I asked.

"Had to go to work early today, so she left at seven. She'll be here when you get home after school. Eat up. Where does your mom keep your lunch bag?"

171

"Second drawer down," I said. I wanted to ask Dad if Mom was mad at him because of Grandpa, but Dad seemed pretty grumpy and I didn't want to make him even more mad. I ate breakfast as fast as I could and went upstairs to brush my teeth.

"Hey, how did you do on that genealogy project?" Dad asked, as he handed me my lunch.

"What project?" I asked, but then I remembered. "Oh, the family one. Right. Yeah. Pretty good. See ya later, Dad. Bye, Dana Scully!!" I grabbed my backpack and ran out the door.

That night Dad didn't come home at all. At least, not while I was awake. And I was awake for a really long time, listening for the garage door to open and Dad's heavy footsteps to come in the house.

Things at home stayed terrible. Mom took extra shifts at Kingsgate Dental, and Dad seemed to find ways to disappear whenever she was home. We weren't allowed to see Grandpa that Sunday either, and that seemed to upset Mom more than the week before. She said that he had caught the flu that was going around the home (to which I say, "well, duh," if you don't open any windows, of course all the flu germs are going to stick around).

All weekend we stayed home, and even though Dad was there we all kind of ignored each other. I took Dana Scully out for super long walks, going past Ali's house several times, but he never saw me. Or if he did he never came out to join me. He was probably hanging out with Tristan. I wanted to believe that he had forgiven me, especially since he was sitting with me again at lunch. But if it wasn't raining he took off fast to the field to play soccer, leaving me to sit alone or go do something else. It was all Tristan's fault. That guy smiled too much and tried too hard to get me to play soccer with them, and I knew it was so that he could show me up on the field. I didn't want anything to do with him, but I pretended to be nice just so that Ali wouldn't ditch me altogether. One lunch hour I made a list of all the things I would do with the money.

CASE: 0024 / FILE: 0009
LOCATION: Vancouver, British Columbia
By Agent Cooper Arcano

USES FOR REWARD MONEY

$200 from bet :

- Buy pencil crayons, pen ink and good paper for Ali

- Buy myself something super cool

With D.B. Cooper reward money:

- Pay for Grandpa's care home

- Pay for Disneyland vacation for family

- Buy second TV (maybe third TV for my room)

- Pay Mom and Dad's bills

- Save some up for later

An exhaustive search of the internet didn't reveal as much as I had hoped about the reward money I could get from the FBI for finding D.B. Cooper, so I couldn't add that to the list.

Considering that the case was technically closed on July 8, 2016, after they spent forty-five years not finding the guy, it's hard to tell what the reward would be. The only thing I saw was that the kid who found the 290 twenty-dollar bills by the river back in 1980 got to keep half of what was left after the FBI kept 14 of the bills as evidence. So, all told, he got $2,760. Then he sold some of it at an auction and got even more money.

That was just for finding some of the money! I imagined what I would get for finding the actual guy! At least double that, I figured. I bet I could even take Ali with us to Disneyland. Ali was going to love that.

The biggest problem was that it ended up being three weeks before we were allowed back to Golden Sunsets. I was worried about my bet with Tristan. There wasn't any time left, and I still only had kind-of proof, not real proof. So far it was okay; I didn't mention it and neither did Tristan. But it was only a matter of time before he brought it up. So when we headed back I was determined to get the information I needed.

***

I'd forgotten what it smelled like inside Golden Sunsets, or maybe it just smelled stronger because of the cleaning and the quarantine. I wrinkled my nose as we entered.

"Just breathe normally. You won't notice it after a minute if you stop focusing on it," Mom snapped. She was unnaturally on edge, or else maybe after having three weeks off I had forgotten how stressed out she got on Sundays. Things around the house had been tense but not as bad, although Dad was barely home anymore. I was just trying to not have her frustration come my way, but it wasn't really working.

She pointed to the hand sanitizer beside the door on our way in. "Use that. I don't want you getting sick too," she said.

When Mom was satisfied with my hand sanitizing, she punched in the door code.

As soon as we entered, one of the nurses noticed us and jumped up. She bustled over our way.

"Ms. Cooke?" she asked.

"Well, Arcano for the last fifteen years, but yes."

"I'm Carrie. I'm one of your dad's caregivers. I wanted to give you a little heads-up about your dad. His mental state has declined quite a bit since getting sick, so I don't want you to be alarmed when you see him today. I think you are meeting with Dr. Choi today as well?"

Mom nodded. "We spoke on the phone yesterday. She said she would be in around two o'clock."

Carrie nodded vigorously. "Great. Great. Okay then. Mr. Cooke is in his room today. He's still recovering from the flu. I'll let Dr. Choi know you're here." She scuttled off, and we went to Grandpa's room. The door was pulled closed, so Mom knocked lightly.

"Hi, Dad. It's your daughter Dawn. I'm here with Cooper, your grandson," she introduced us both as we entered.

I gasped when I saw Grandpa. He was still in bed, with the covers thrown off. He had only pyjama pants on, no shirt. He looked like he weighed less than me, he was so skinny. He was drinking apple juice out of a plastic cup and straw, which made him look like an old man pretending to be a toddler. His eyes narrowed when Mom went up and gave him a kiss on the cheek.

"We've been worried about you, Dad. You had the flu, so we couldn't visit. I missed you," Mom said.

Grandpa grunted in response.

"Cooper has been working on a school project about you and Mom. It's been great to relive some memories of being a kid. Mom's name was Linda. It's nice to think about Linda, isn't it?"

I hung back at the door while Mom nattered at Grandpa, who occasionally grunted or said words in response, but never put together a sentence. There was no way that I was going to be able to interrogate Grandpa in this state. I didn't even want to look at him. I studied the photo of Grandma and Grandpa's wedding, hoping that maybe there would be a clue or a hint in the background — anything that would help my case. He looked so strong and healthy in the old photo. Looking at the half-naked guy in the bed in front of me, it was hard to put these two different versions of my grandfather into one person.

Dr. Choi came into Grandpa's room a few minutes after two. She was short, shorter than me, but she scared me. She seemed like my principal when she came into our class unannounced.

"Mrs. Cooke-Arcano. Nice to see you again. I take it this is your son?" she said, nodding my direction. I nodded back and carefully put the photo on the top of the bookshelf. Then I backed away even more.

"Perhaps he would be more comfortable waiting outside? Then you and I and Mr. Cooke can have a little chat between grown-ups." Then she turned to me, and her voice went up an octave. "It'll be pretty boring stuff for you. I'm sure you'd rather watch TV in the lounge. How's that sound?"

Oh, I hated her now, acting like I was a kid even though I was practically a teenager. But I definitely didn't want to hang around with her in the room, so I nodded.

"Yeah. sure. I'll be either in the lounge or outside, Mom," I said. "I'll see you later, Grandpa."

It didn't really matter if I said hello or goodbye to him, but I knew Mom would chastise me on manners if I didn't acknowledge that I was leaving.

As I expected, there was no response from Grandpa anyway. I left the room and heard Dr. Choi start talking about the weather as I pulled the door shut behind me.

I wandered into the lounge, but I didn't feel like being inside. I looked for Mrs. Kim. It had been so long since I had seen her and I wanted to make it up to her for upsetting her the last time. But she was nowhere to be found.

The TV was on some old western movie, and one old lady was clasping the remote like it was a teddy bear, so there was no way I could change the channel. Nothing was going my way today. I slumped into an empty recliner and pretended to watch TV.

I must have fallen asleep, because Mom shook me awake to go home.

"Grandpa has to move," Mom said, emotionless, when we got into the car. "When he got the flu it took a lot out of him, and he's declined a lot since our last visit. Golden Sunsets isn't set up for the care that he needs."

"Oh," I said.

"I'm going to talk to your dad and Auntie Jane and see if we can get him moved in the next few weeks. Dr. Choi has already made some preliminary calls to find a proper place for him that can provide the care he needs. There's a place in Vancouver, which will be nice, not having to drive to Ladner every week. Dr. Choi said they have an opening, but we have to move fast." Mom sounded kind of robotic.

"Yeah, that's good," I replied.

"I'm going to try and check it out on my lunch break tomorrow. Talk to the staff."

"Sure," I said.

She sighed and said to herself, "It's gonna be expensive."

I was trying to figure out Grandpa's plan. I was sure he was faking, but this was a bit much. He must be such a good actor, I thought, to be able to seem so out of it. Was it better for him to be in Vancouver? Were the Feds onto him, so he had to move? Things must be getting desperate to pretend not to know words anymore or to hurt his own family. What was he up to?

CHAPTER 24

I hung out in my room most of that night, trying to come up with American Marmot stories I could use as conversation starters with Ali the next day. I couldn't come up with much: all of my ideas were either about D.B. Cooper or involved a psycho with an exploding soccer ball who looked a lot like Tristan. Neither was going to work.

When I came out before bed to get a glass of water, Mom was sitting in the kitchen with Dana Scully dozing on her lap. She was staring at her empty notebook of Grandpa's stories, tapping her pen on the page absentmindedly. I sat down across from her. She smiled weakly at me.

"Mom, can I ask you a question? How come you have to pay for Grandpa? Doesn't he have enough money?"

Mom closed her notebook and sighed. "It's complicated. Nothing you have to worry about, that's for sure," she said. "How did your comic drawing go? Come up with any great superheroes?"

"Not really. It's not as fun without Ali."

"How is Ali? How come you don't invite him over anymore?"

I wanted to remind her that I was grounded, but she was right. Ali never came over, even before then. He hadn't been over since the summer. I didn't tell her that I didn't want him to hear my parents fighting. I didn't tell her that I didn't even want to be here most of the time for the same reason.

"He's been playing soccer a lot, and prefers hanging out with those guys," I said. It came out sounding more upset than I expected. It was also true, though, I realized.

"Honey, I'm sorry. It's hard when your best friend and you go separate ways."

"We're not going our separate ways!" I said. "It's just soccer season!"

"Okay, okay. I'm sorry. I'm glad to hear it too. I like Ali. He's a good egg." She yawned and stretched. "I'm going to go to bed early, I think. You should too."

"Yeah, I am. Good night," I said. I picked up Dana Scully and went to my room. I was mad about Mom's comment, but it wasn't worth getting into it. I closed the door and sank down behind it.

Ali and I weren't going our separate ways, were we? Was this the slow death of our best friendship? Tristan and Ali had soccer and camp and video games and stuff that happened in their class to talk about. Ali and I had comics and *The X-Files*.

Was it enough? What if Ali liked Tristan more? Tristan probably didn't have parents who fought all the time. I bet he never even got grounded. Tristan had money too, and if I didn't solve this case we were going to be super poor and my parents would be divorced and I would have to move into an apartment and they probably wouldn't allow dogs so I'd have to get rid of Dana Scully and I'd have to go to a new school and no one there would like me.

I couldn't help it. I started crying, burying my face into Dana Scully's soft fur. I could lose everything if I lost this bet — my best friend, my parents, my money, my house, probably even my dog.

**

The Friday before Grandpa's moving day, Mom picked me up from school and I went with her to make sure that everything was ready at the new, equally lame-named care home, "Memory Lane." I thought it was a terrible name, considering that the people who live there don't have memories, but I could see how a bunch of business people would think it was perfect.

"I don't know why I have to go," I said.

"You don't. You can stay in the car if you want. I just want to pop in and make sure everything's ready," Mom replied, as we pulled into the garage below the building.

Staying in the car sounded boring too, which I think Mom knew, because she had a little smile on her face when I sighed and got out of the car.

It felt like we were trying to enter Alcatraz. There was a high fence surrounding the place, with a buzzer to the front desk just to get access to the parking lot. Inside we had to stop and get buzzed in every few doors — once to get into the parking garage, once to get into the elevator to go up from the parking garage, once to get out of the elevator vestibule and into the actual place.

I felt nervous while we checked in. I didn't know what to expect. There were photos of old movie stars on the walls, but overall it felt way more like a hospital than Grandpa's old place. I stayed close to Mom's side, and I even thought about holding her hand as we walked down the hall behind the admin lady to get to Grandpa's new room.

It was a lot smaller than his last room, with just a hospital bed on one side and nothing else. "There's no TV," I said aloud to Mom.

"We'll bring the one he has," Mom replied. "It'll be better once we have his chair and dresser in here."

"Once those are in here, there'll be no room for people," I said. Mom ignored me.

The walls were painted a horrible green colour. It also smelled funny, like the bathroom garbage can hadn't been emptied in a while, and the smell took over the whole room, wafting in and out. I tried to open the window, but it was bolted shut. Not that Grandpa would have had a view anyway; the window looked straight onto the next wing, with only a view of red brick and more closed windows.

Mom looked around while I hung back in the doorway.

"Looks clean!" Mom exclaimed with a fake brightness in her voice. "Let's go see the rest. Poke around a bit."

I followed her around like Dana Scully follows me, watching while Mom poked her nose into different open doors and little alcoves, each time saying "oh, that's cute" or "this will be a nice place for us to chat on our visits" or "Grandpa loved John Wayne movies; he'll get a kick out of this John Wayne wall."

All I could see was how horrible this place was. There was no carpet in the hallways. The alcoves had comfy-looking chairs, but there was no one using any of them; the John Wayne wall was four photos probably printed off the internet and put in dollar-store frames; and the whole place stank. The worst part was the eating area.

We had arrived at four thirty, so dinner was in full force. Old people must get hungry early. The room was full of people in wheelchairs. Most of them were not eating. I counted five staff members, each trying to feed two people at a time, turning from one to the next, holding spoons to their mouths like they were feeding giant babies. The food looked like baby food too, all separated on divider plates. For a room full of people, it was silent except for the murmuring whispers of the staff coaxing people to eat and the scrape of cutlery on plates.

"I gotta go," I said, and walked away as quickly as I could. I practically ran to the reception area and locked myself in the washroom. I stayed in there for a long time, sitting on the counter beside the sink. I didn't want to see any more of Memory Lane. In fact, I wanted to forget Memory Lane existed.

There was a knock on the door. "Cooper? Are you in there?"

"Yeah." I opened the door and faced my mom. "Why are you putting Grandpa in here? He's not as bad as all these other people."

Mom's shoulders tensed up. "Hon, he is. He will be. We're making decisions for the future."

"Why? Would you want to live here?" I asked her.

"I'm not sick like Grandpa," she said.

"Yeah, but would you want to live here? When you're old like Grandpa, do you want me to put you in a place like this?" I was getting upset, and I hated getting upset, which actually made me more upset.

"This isn't about us, Cooper. This is the best place for your grandpa to be. They have lots of great staff, and doctors here all the time. This is necessary. I know it's hard to understand, but—"

I cut her off. "I'm not a kid, Mom. I understand that Grandpa is sick. What I don't understand is why you would take him from one sucky place to another. This place is total crap!"

I said it loudly, loud enough that my mother grabbed me by the shoulder and moved me forcibly toward the elevator vestibule. She punched in the key code, still holding my shoulder with the other hand. I shrugged her off once we were in the locked box waiting for the elevator to come.

Normally I would just let it go, but I couldn't. Neither D.B. Cooper nor Fox Mulder would sit back and stay silent.

"It's not the best place, Mom. It stinks. It's small. All the people in there are blobs. Putting Grandpa with them is just going to turn him into a blob too! He should be with the nice Alzheimer's people! He used to be nice, remember? He always gave me money and we got ice cream. He made jokes. He should be hanging out with people like Mrs. Kim. He would be nicer if he was with nice people. Maybe he would be better too. Mrs. Kim isn't as bad as he is, and I bet it's because she lives at home!"

"Cooper Arcano! That is enough."

The elevator arrived and I threw myself inside, which did not help my situation. I wanted to be able to storm off, but instead I was stuck. I faced the wall, away from my mother.

She was silent behind me. When the door opened on the garage level I rushed out of the elevator first, although then I had to wait for her to punch in the code again to get out of the elevator room to the garage itself. I was braced for her to yell back, but she didn't say anything to me the whole ride home, which was worse. I stared out the car window, but I couldn't help but look over at her every once in a while, just to make sure that she knew I was still mad. But she didn't look at me. She just watched the road, and she looked so, so tired.

By the time we got home, I knew that I had to act now. I didn't know which was worse, but I was pretty sure that putting Grandpa in the blob house was the worst thing. He would hate it. Really, I was doing him a favour by turning him in.

CHAPTER 25

CASE: 0024 / FILE: 0010
LOCATION: Vancouver, British Columbia

Dear FBI,

I, Cooper Arcano, am an aspiring FBI agent, and I believe I have cracked your most famous unsolved case: the D.B. Cooper file.

There are still holes, so my case is not rock-solid; however, there are now time constraints on my investigation of the case. The suspect is about to be sent to ~~the blob house~~ a new, highly guarded facility, where any chance of interrogating him will be lost.

My suspect is Bartholomew Donald Cooke. He matches the description of D.B. Cooper and had a solid motive for skyjacking a plane. I have enclosed photos of ~~my grandfather~~ the suspect, B.D. Cooke, alongside versions of the composite drawings of D.B. Cooper in 1971 and the imagined portraits of what D.B. Cooper would look like today. Please note how similar he looks in both versions. He even has the same sunglasses on in the photo from 1978!

I have also uncovered the following:

The suspect owns a tie clip similar to the one on the tie left on the plane by D.B. Cooper.

The suspect has American money from 1970 and 1971.

The suspect was in love with a Canadian, which was basically illegal back then.

The suspect was in the navy, and was possibly in the paratrooper unit.

I have included all of the case files from my investigation. Remember, the suspect is old and about to be unreachable in many ways, so I strongly encourage you to take me seriously. I look forward to hearing from you and receiving my reward, but you'll have to come to Vancouver (the one in Canada, not the one in Washington).

Yours truly,
Cooper Arcano
Future Agent

Once I had composed my letter to the FBI, I felt better. I printed it off and looked over my shoulder. Dana Scully was lying in the middle of the room. I was positive she was giving me a disapproving look.

"What?" I said. She put her head down, facing away from me.

"It's for the best," I explained. "They aren't going to put him in jail. They'll get permission to come to Canada to meet him, and they'll probably put him in a hotel while they question him. He's so famous. Famous people stay in fancy hotels, not in tiny hospital rooms. And they're the FBI, which means that they have really amazing doctors who can probably help Grandpa access his D.B. Cooper memories too. I mean, if he is actually sick." Dana Scully sighed.

"I just don't think the blob house is good for him. And Mom said it's really expensive. If he's faking, he would be really upset to know that his daughter is paying for somewhere he doesn't really need." I paused. "I bet the FBI will want to know about how he did it. And we need the reward money. You've heard Mom and Dad."

Dana Scully got up and left the room. I knew my reasons kind of sucked. I think Dana Scully thought the money was for my own benefit. But what did she know? She's just a dog.

I put my letter in an envelope, and then realized that I would have to put all my files in too. I looked at my crime board. It was way too big to fit in an envelope.

After some searching I was able to find Dad's old digital camera, so I took photos of my crime board. I made sure to zoom in and get all the parts of the board and how they connected. I printed them off. Our printer was really old, so everything came out kind of purple, but it was good enough. Once I was sure that everything the FBI would need was in the envelope, I slid my letter in. Now all I needed was an address and a stamp. I wondered if I should send it to a specific person. The FBI probably got letters all the time, but if I could find the name of an FBI agent it would show that I was serious. I would look into that later, when I had more time with the computer.

I figured that I would have time to mail it during the move. I asked Mom if I could stay home while they were moving Grandpa, but she said no, I needed to be there to keep Grandpa company.

"He doesn't need my company. He doesn't know who I am," I said. "Can I at least have my tablet back if I'm going to be stuck there the whole day?"

"It shouldn't take the whole day, Cooper. It's only a bit of furniture. Plus, I could probably use your help packing his closet and dresser."

"I'm not touching his underwear," I stated.

"That's fine. You're still coming. Don't you want to say goodbye to Mrs. Ken?"

"It's Mrs. Kim, Mom. Not Mrs. Ken."

"Right, sorry. Mrs. Kim. You can see her, and you can pack and talk to Grandpa. Plus, maybe you'll want some of his books or knick-knacks. We won't have room for all of them in his new room. I need your help picking which ones to bring," she said. "We're going to leave in half an hour, once your dad gets back from the gym. Be ready."

I sighed loudly and went upstairs to change. I took my backpack and put the envelope inside. I could ask for the WiFi password to look up FBI-agent addresses, or maybe there would be a nice nurse-receptionist who would give me a stamp and mail it for me. I went over my crime board one more time to ensure that I had included everything I needed to. Did I need to include the motive? I didn't know how to add that in, so I quickly forged a love letter from my grandfather to my grandmother:

Roses are red
Planes fly high
I can't wait to see you on
The Canadian side

It wasn't my best work, but I thought that it wasn't too terrible, so I threw it in the envelope.

On our way out the door I grabbed my tablet from the desk drawer where Mom had held it hostage.

The ride over was the first time we had been in a car as a family in a long time. I wondered if this was the moment they would tell me they were getting divorced, since there was nowhere I could go, but instead Dad just turned up the radio so that no one could talk.

When we got to Golden Sunsets, Grandpa was confused, as always, but he seemed more on edge than normal. He was fully dressed, even ready to go outside with a jacket and loafers. He was pacing around the hallway, muttering to himself and fiddling with his wallet.

"I'll get started," Dad said to Mom, going into Grandpa's room. I peeked in and saw that someone had already put empty boxes on the floor and spread his clothes out on the bed.

Mom took Grandpa by the elbow and led him to the common room. I followed her.

"Dad, you just stay here and relax. Marco and I are going to pack up and then we'll head over to the new place. It's so close to our place in Vancouver! I'll be able to visit even more!" She turned to me. "Can you stay and watch Grandpa?" I nodded. Mom headed down the hall.

Grandpa stood up quickly and started pacing again. "I have to go," he declared.

"Yeah, Grandpa. We will. But Mom and Dad have to pack first."

"Now! Go!" he said loudly. He was agitated and getting angry.

"Where do you want to go?" I asked.

"Find. Find . . ." he stammered.

My interest was piqued. "Find what?"

"Find. Find . . ." he repeated, wringing his hands and gesturing. He walked up to the door and looked out.

"No go, Grandpa. We're both grounded," I said. He looked at the nurse-receptionist, who looked up from her phone and shook her head no at him. He grunted and continued pacing, then he threw himself into the armchair closest to the door and stared. I watched as he closed his eyes and fell asleep.

I dropped my backpack beside him and pulled out my tablet to play something. Just as I was getting started the door opened. Mr. and Mrs. Kim entered together. I put the tablet back in my bag and stood up.

"Hi, Mrs. Kim!" I smiled at her, and Mr. Kim smiled back at me tiredly. Mrs. Kim looked at me like she could almost place how she knew me.

"I'm Cooper. We have been working on a mystery together. And I was hoping I would see you today, because I think we solved it!"

"Mmmhmm?" Mrs. Kim had this look on her face like she was humouring me. I knew it well; my parents used it a lot.

"You were very helpful," I said.

"Mmmhmm," she repeated.

"Sorry, Cooper. It's been a bit of a day for us. Yireh is going to be moving in here this week. A space has opened up and we decided it was the best thing for both of us," Mr. Kim explained. "Maybe you'll get to solve some other mysteries when she's here full-time."

"Oh," I said. I realized Mrs. Kim was probably moving into Grandpa's room. It made me sad to think about losing her too. "No. My grandpa is moving out today. I guess this is it, then." I felt deflated.

Mr. Kim patted my shoulder. "It's tough, isn't it? We find it tough too." His kindness almost made me cry, totally out of nowhere.

"I guess I thought she would be okay," I said. "It was dumb to think that, probably."

"Not dumb at all. She's a trouper, this one.

We like to joke that if anyone can forget to have Alzheimer's, it'll be Yireh." I kind of laughed with him.

"I'm pretty sure I know which room will be hers," I said. "I can show you."

"That would be great, Cooper. Thanks," Mr. Kim said. "We'll miss seeing you around here. I know Yireh always enjoyed chatting with the 'handsome young man' when she was here."

I smiled weakly. "I liked talking with her too."

I led Mr. and Mrs. Kim to Grandpa's room. Mom and Dad were both in the closet, dropping things into boxes. Mom was folding every jacket and sweater perfectly, and Dad was rolling things into balls and shoving them into the boxes we had brought. Most of the room was done, and boxes were stacked in three piles.

"I bet this will be your room," I said to Mrs. Kim. Mom and Dad startled at the sound of my voice.

"Cooper! We didn't see you there! Where's Grandpa?" Mom said.

"Sleeping," I said. "Mrs. Kim is going to be moving in here," I explained to Mom.

"Oh . . . well. It's an excellent facility," she said to Mr. Kim politely, then she turned to me. "While you're here, do you want to go through the top box there? We're going to give most of that pile to Goodwill, but there might be some stuff you want to keep."

I shrugged apologetically at Mr. and Mrs. Kim, who shuffled backwards and out of the room. I followed them and we stood awkwardly in the hall. I didn't know if it was because Mrs. Kim recognized Grandpa's room, but she seemed to perk up. "Mysteries!" She almost shouted the word.

I grinned. "Yeah! Mysteries! We talked about them sometimes. Like those books."

"I have a book for you!" She rummaged around in her purse and pulled out a lipstick. Mr. Kim gently took it from her hand, and Mrs. Kim frowned.

"How about we mail the book to Cooper?" he said, and she smiled. Mr. Kim handed me his phone and asked me to put my address into it.

"We do have a book for you. I'll send it along," Mr. Kim said, patting Mrs. Kim's hand.

"Cooper!" Mom hollered from inside Grandpa's closet.

I gave Mr. Kim his phone and went back into the room.

CHAPTER 26

I sat down on Grandpa's bed and looked inside the box Mom had left there. It was mostly knick-knack type stuff, like Grandpa's mallard-duck statue and the fake Fabergé egg. I took out both of these things and put them aside. I thought we could put them on the mantel. Most of the rest was *National Geographic* magazines, so I left them in the box and hefted it down off the bed onto the floor.

"Make sure you put that away from the other stuff. The boxes close to the door are going to the new place, and the ones by the bookshelf are going to our house," Dad said.

"What on earth?" Mom had pulled down one of the back shoeboxes and hidden behind it was a small lockbox. It was exactly like the one Grandpa had given me for Christmas a few years ago!

"Ooh, the mystery never ends," Dad said. "A lockbox. Do you know the code to open it?" He stopped and leaned over Mom's shoulder.

"Probably 0305. That's the code he used for

everything," she said. Mom punched in the numbers and pulled out a bunch of papers, photos and money.

0305? That was D.B. Cooper's flight number!

"What is it?" I asked, trying to see into the box.

"Looks like a bunch of junk," Dad announced, and went back to rolling clothes and putting them into the boxes.

"Can I see?"

"Sure." Mom handed over the box and the papers. I grabbed the photos and looked at each one. Most of them were of Grandpa and Grandma; Grandma was pregnant in some of them. And a few of a baby that must have been Mom or Auntie Jane. I handed them to Mom after I shuffled through. There was an invitation from Mom and Dad's wedding in the box, which I handed over as well.

I picked up the money. It was all American dollar bills. I looked for the year they were printed, but most of them were from the nineties and two thousands.

"Hey, finders keepers," Dad said, when he saw me examining the money. "That's your mother's inheritance in that safe."

"It's not that much," I said, putting it back.

As I did that, though, I noticed something at the bottom of the empty box. I pulled out the paper. It was well worn, the paper feeling almost like fabric, so I had to be really careful not to tear it as I opened it up.

It was an old road map of Washington State.

There were some small holes in the paper where there were corners in the folds. I flattened the map out on the floor to get a closer look.

Someone had put six little blue stars on the map. Marked locations! I put my finger on each one. Ariel. Mount St. Helens. Elmer City. Just outside of Vancouver, Washington (I still couldn't get over that someone thought it was a good idea to name two cities that are super close together the same thing). Olympia, which upon further investigation was just marking the capital city. Chelan Falls. There was also a tiny "X" on Leavenworth.

My mind was blown. Had I just discovered the map marking the spots where D.B. Cooper had hidden his money? It made sense. Some D.B. Cooper experts said that he landed in Ariel. Money was found on Tena Bar by Vancouver, Washington, in 1980. Mount St. Helens erupted in 1980, so any money that was there would be deeply buried now. It was very possible that Grandpa had hidden the $200,000 along the way to Canada, thinking he would come back later to get it. But then he never returned because they changed the rules at the border or something.

It was smart. You should never hide all your money in one place, in case it gets discovered. Ali taught me that because his sister sometimes came into his room without asking, and once she "borrowed" a ten-dollar bill he had in his desk drawer. From then on, he always hid everything separately.

What was the best thing to do now? Was it better to hold on to the map and try to find the money myself? Or should I send it into the FBI with the rest of my case files? I traced the map with my finger and followed the Columbia River from Ariel all the way up to the border by Trail and Castlegar in British Columbia. Was this how Grandpa got into Canada? Or did he come up along the coast? If he was in the navy, maybe he took a boat and entered through international waters. There were so many things that I wanted to know about the transformation from D.B. Cooper into my own grandfather. How did he do it?

I folded up the map again and put it in the pocket of my hoodie. I could take a photo of it and add it to my crime board. This had to be the proof I had been looking for!

Meanwhile, Mom had gotten caught up in the photos. She was studying each one for a long time, and then carefully putting them on the bed.

"I'm going to put these in the scrapbook," she said. "Grandpa won't remember that these were in the closet."

"He won't remember that his money was in here too," Dad said. "Should we take it and run?"

Mom swatted him with the photos. "Marco!"

"Kidding! I'm totally kidding!"

I stood up and looked around. "I'm going back to Grandpa," I said.

This was my chance to interrogate him one-on-

one about the map and the flight. I was confident I could get the truth out of him now!

"We should be done soon, hon," Mom said. "Maybe another half hour, hour, then we'll need your help getting stuff into Dad's truck. I know it kind of sucks, but we'll go for pizza or something tonight. I promise."

"No prob," I said, and I walked out.

I looked around for my grandfather, but he wasn't in the chair where he had fallen asleep. I scanned the room. He wasn't anywhere I could see. I assumed he was in the bathroom, but when the toilet flushed and the door opened, it wasn't him.

The nurse-receptionist was doing something on her cellphone and turned away from the door so that her power cord reached the outlet. There were a few other residents watching TV, and Mr. and Mrs. Kim were sitting at a table by the window.

I walked over to them. "Hi," I said. "Have you seen my grandfather? He was sleeping right there before and now he's not there."

Mr. Kim shook his head. "Have you checked the lunchroom?"

I thanked him and walked down the hall, past the bedrooms, to the dining area. There were a couple of cleaning staff setting up for dinner, but no sign of Grandpa.

I went back to the common room. He wasn't there. He wasn't anywhere. Then I looked down beside the chairs. My backpack was gone too.

CHAPTER 27

I didn't know what to do. Grandpa was missing and so was my D.B. Cooper case file. He knew! He knew that I was onto him, and he stole my backpack and disappeared.

From everything I had learned about D.B. Cooper, I knew he would be good at hiding. He had hidden from the FBI for fifty years. I was so angry. How could I fall for such an easy ruse as falling asleep? And how stupid was I to leave my backpack full of all the evidence with a known criminal? What was I supposed to do now?

I looked around the room again, but I knew that Grandpa was not in the building anymore. He had gotten past the nurse-receptionist, snuck out, and was probably off to reclaim his riches and live a whole new life. He had been faking this whole time, and we fell for it.

I left the ward and stormed outside. I had to find him. I was the one who uncovered him, and I wasn't going to let him get away this easy.

I looked around Golden Sunsets, but I couldn't see Grandpa anywhere. I ran around the building, but he wasn't there either. He had definitely walked away. I just had to decide where. I only really knew a bit about Ladner, and I didn't have any idea where we were in relation to the downtown area I went to with Ali. I walked out to the street and looked both ways. No visual on Grandpa. The street was quiet, and I knew that when we drove here we came from the right. That led to the highway. I went that way.

I guess I wasn't ever really paying too much attention on the drive to Ladner, because I thought there was only a few turns when we got off the highway to get to Golden Sunsets. But I walked to the end of the block and didn't recognize anything.

I crossed the street and walked straight for another block. There was a school on the other side of the street. I had never noticed passing a school before. I turned right, away from the school and onto a smaller street with houses along it. I found myself in a cul-de-sac. Left was also a cul-de-sac. I went back to the school to start again.

I needed to think this through. The only thing I had with me was a map of Washington, so that wasn't going to get me anywhere. I had to change mindsets. I had to think like D.B. Cooper. I had to think like Grandpa. Which way would he go?

D.B. Cooper made up his mind and he went with it. I assumed my D.B. Cooper personality from drama class, and I walked with purpose past the school and onward.

After the school I continued straight on my path. I needed to get my case file. I needed to find my suspect. Then I realized that I was both D.B. Cooper AND Fox Mulder. Criminal and FBI agent. I chuckled to myself, then ran the next two blocks.

I could hear the highway from where I was standing; it was definitely close, so I felt like I was on the right track. D.B. Cooper would be drawn to where there were more people, in order to blend in. I ran toward the highway sounds, but there was a giant wall between me and the actual roadway. I looked right and left. Down the way there was a set of stairs leading to the pedestrian overpass. I headed toward that.

While I was walking I kept looking for clues too. I was shocked at how much money I found; I was $1.60 richer by the time I got to the top of the overpass. I also found a shiny ball that definitely could be part of a tie clip.

I crossed over the highway. The overpass was really high; it made my stomach feel queasy to look over the side. I would never be like D.B. Cooper. Even with a parachute, jumping from high up would be terrifying! I couldn't see Grandpa from my bird's-eye view, despite being able to look over the giant wall and see a lot of the neighbourhood streets. He had gotten farther than I thought.

I walked down the other side of the overpass.

I recognized the field that was near the bus loop, and I could even see the golden arches of the McDonald's on the other side.

Then I remembered: Mom had mentioned something about Grandpa and that McDonald's. He used to go with Grandma every day. He wouldn't be able to resist stopping there for nostalgia's sake. I could catch up to him there and demand my backpack of evidence back — and be a hero for finding him. I set my course and headed over.

It took a really long time to walk there. It looked so much shorter from up above. I decided to use my new-found money to get fries at McDonald's while Grandpa and I waited for backup to come get us. I picked up a few more dimes along the way.

I thought about what I was going to say to Grandpa when I found him. I was going to tell him about how I was onto him, that I knew he was D.B. Cooper, that I knew he was faking his Alzheimer's, and to give back my case file.

"What's your next step, Grandpa?" I would ask him. "To get the rest of the hidden money?! Because I know where that is too!" And I would show him the map, at which point he would break down and beg me to keep his secret, promise that he would pay me any amount of money to help him get away.

Would I help him in that case? I thought about it. How much money would it take to buy my silence? This wasn't all about the money, I thought, this was also about justice and trust. We were family.

If you can't trust your family with your biggest secrets, who can you trust?

It felt like it was over an hour of walking to get to the McDonald's. I looked around for Grandpa, but he wasn't there. I had missed him. I swore under my breath and went up to the counter.

"Hey, can I get a large glass of water and a small fries, please?"

The girl behind the counter blinked excessively at me. "That all?"

"Well, actually, have you seen an old guy in here lately? He would have been alone, carrying a red backpack and wearing, like, a yellow jacket? White-grey hair? Tall-ish?"

She blinked at me more. It was very off-putting. "Nope," she said.

"Are you sure? He probably came here," I said.

"Nope." She blinked some more. I squinted and moved in. Was she trying to tell me something in Morse code with her blinking? But she just blinked more and then turned away to get my fries.

I turned to the guy next to her. "Did you see an old guy with a backpack? Looks like me maybe, but, like, seventy years older?"

The guy looked at me like I was crazy. "Nah. Just families mostly today," he replied.

I picked up my fries and drink and sat down facing the street. I contemplated my next move. Where else would he have gone?

Then I knew it! The filing cabinet! He was

going to get something out of storage. Or maybe he thought that the map was in there and not in the lockbox Mom found at Golden Sunsets. And now I had the map with me. That was it. He was at Auntie Elena's construction-rental place.

I shoved the last few fries into my mouth and washed them down with the water. Then I headed out, a renewed vigour and D.B. Cooper attitude surrounding me.

CHAPTER 28

It was another twenty-five minutes to walk to Auntie Eyeliner's work, but I knew where I was now, and I knew how long it would take. I walked briskly along Ladner Trunk Road, making sure to look down each of the side streets to see if Grandpa was hiding. Once he got stuff out of storage, he would probably head to the States to get his money. Ladner is close to Point Roberts, but that was an actual border crossing. No way that he could get across a regular border. I didn't think he even had a passport. D.B. Cooper hadn't needed any ID to get on the plane, so I assumed you didn't need a passport to cross the border back in the seventies. I had no idea how to get to the border, so I was counting on finding him first.

I strode into Double R Rentals like I owned the place, D.B. Cooper style. I nodded at Raffi and looked around for Auntie Eyeliner. I was in luck; just as I came in, she came out from the back.

"Raf, can you double-check the— Cooper!"

"Hi, Auntie Elena," I said.

"Another visit? What a surprise!" She smiled at me. "Is your dad with you?"

"No, I'm supposed to meet my grandpa here. Have you seen him?" I asked. I added on as soon as she raised her eyebrow at me, "My mom and dad are just at his place right now."

Her raised eyebrow went even higher. "I thought your grandpa was sick."

"Well, yeah. We were going to get something else from his stuff," I added. "I mean, add something to it. He wanted to add this." I pulled out the map.

She shook her head. "I think we should call your mom or dad. You shouldn't be here alone. Where is your mom?"

I ignored her. "Has my grandfather been here? This is pretty important. I couldn't find him this morning and we have important business here."

"Let's call your mom together," she said. She grabbed the phone from behind the desk and put it on the top counter.

"What's the number?" she asked me.

"Fine. I'll call her. I don't need your help. I'm not a baby," I said to her.

She stood beside me while I dialled our home number, knowing no one was there.

I let it ring. "No one's home," I said.

"Call her cell," she instructed. I sighed loudly and hung up. I dialled Mom's cell number.

"Hello?!" Mom sounded frantic on the other end.

"Mom? It's me, Cooper," I said.

"It's him! Oh, thank God, it's him!" I heard her say to the room behind her. "Cooper, where are you? Are you okay? Are you with Grandpa? Are you okay?"

"I'm at Auntie Eye . . . Auntie Elena's work. I was looking for Grandpa and I thought he might be here," I explained. "I'm totally fine, but Grandpa's not here." At this point, Raffi called out from the backroom, so Auntie Eyeliner mussed my hair and walked away.

"What . . . why . . . what . . . you know what? Stay there. Your dad is coming to get you," Mom said. "Stay there. I love you. Stay there. Don't . . . just stay there. Okay. Dad's on his way."

I hung up and waited outside for Dad to come. There was no sign of Grandpa anyway. I was out of ideas. Where could he have gone? How did he get away so fast? Maybe he went straight to the border. Or maybe he had an accomplice, maybe someone was waiting for him outside Golden Sunsets to whisk him away to a new life. I imagined all the different scenarios until I saw my dad's truck zoom into the parking lot.

He pulled up beside me and was jumping out before it even fully stopped.

"Cooper!" He pulled me into an awkward bear hug. "Where the hell did you go?"

"I was looking for Grandpa. I thought he would be here. I checked the McDonald's too," I said.

"Buddy, we thought you were abducted! You can't just leave like that! Your mother is going out of her mind right now! Losing you and Don?!" He pulled me in tighter and swore a few more times.

"Sorry." My voice was muffled by Dad's flannel shirt.

"Let's go back. Your mom is waiting to smother you to death," Dad said.

"You're doing a pretty good job yourself," I mumbled into his chest.

He let me go and we got into the truck.

As we drove back, Dad looked over at me. "Why would you think Grandpa would be at Elena's?"

"To get his stuff from storage?" I answered. "Or maybe there's something valuable there that he wants."

"Cooper, Don isn't with it. He doesn't remember that he has stuff in storage, much less where it would be. He doesn't even know Elena exists," Dad said. "Half the time he doesn't even know his own name."

"Maybe he's faking," I mumbled, as we pulled up at Golden Sunsets.

Dad put the truck in park. "What?"

I was silent, not repeating what I said.

"Cooper, look at me." I avoided his eyes and focused on Dad's shirt. "Buddy, look at me."

"I just don't think he really lost all his memories.

I think Grandpa knows stuff. He's faking. He's got secrets," I said, in a low voice.

Dad wasn't getting out of the truck. "Cooper. You're a smart kid. And I know it's tough to see your grandpa like this. Even I would prefer to have my jackass of a father-in-law back too. This is not him, and we have to help him and we have to help your mom. He's not going to get better. And, buddy, it sucks. It really does, but trust me when I say that he's not faking."

At this point, I hate to admit it, but I started crying. It was very un–D.B. Cooper of me.

CHAPTER 29

There were two cops at Golden Sunsets, standing in the lobby with Mom. The hug I got from her was fierce and protective, and she wouldn't let go, even after I asked her to. I rolled my eyes at one of the cops, but I didn't get even a hint of a smile from her.

"One out of two," Dad announced.

"I was looking for Grandpa. I looked at McDonald's," I said to the cops from Mom's embrace. "He wasn't there. He also wasn't anywhere between here and Auntie Eyeliner's place."

Mom repeated what I said. "You looked at McDonald's."

"Yeah, because he went there with Grandma," I explained, but Mom just hugged me harder.

"Next time you tell a grown-up before you head out, okay, son? Your parents were worried sick," the cop said.

I rolled my eyes (in my head this time) and nodded again. "Sorry."

"We've put out the alert around the lower

mainland for your father, so hopefully we'll get a bite soon," the cop said to Mom. "The hardest part now is waiting. Can we get you a coffee or something?"

Mom shook her head.

I thought about whether I should tell them my theory, but they probably wouldn't take me seriously. Then I remembered: Grandpa had my backpack.

"Grandpa has my backpack with him," I said.

The adults all looked over at me. I shrugged. "At least, I think he does. I left it beside the chair he was in, and it was gone when he went missing. It has my tablet in it."

"Was your tablet turned on?" the cop asked.

I nodded. "Yeah. I mean, it was in sleep mode, but it's still on."

"Great. That's actually great. We may be able to track it," she said. "Give me a minute. I'm going to see what we can do." She left us, already calling someone on her radio.

Mom and Dad both looked at me, and I felt like maybe my "we were so worried and we love you so much" moments were up, and we were headed into the "what were you thinking, I told you to leave the tablet at home, and you're so grounded" lecture.

But before either of them could start, the policewoman was back. "It looks like we're able to track your son's tablet, but I'm going to need some information from you. Are all your devices linked through a family account?"

Mom looked over at Dad, who nodded. "They sure are. What do we need?"

Suddenly all the adults were in action mode, jogging off to log in to cloud accounts and provide numbers and GPS information and who knows what else. I was left alone in the lobby, but not before Mom turned back to me and said, "Stay there."

I lay down on the bench, suddenly exhausted. But I didn't have time to have a nap, because moments later the flurry returned.

"They've found him!" Mom exclaimed.

"Boundary Bay!" Dad added. "Close to the airport!"

"OF COURSE!" I shouted. How could I miss even considering the airport? It was the most logical place of all!

Mom, Dad and I followed the cop car toward the airport in Dad's truck. Mom was talking fast, blaming herself for everything, and Dad was trying to console her. I was in the back seat, trying to figure out how Grandpa got that far. I couldn't believe I missed the connection. Of course he would go to the smaller airport. Security would be less strict, and it would easier to get on a plane.

But Grandpa wasn't actually anywhere close to the airport. The cops saw him first and pulled over on the side of the road. He was sitting on the ground, and he looked upset. Mom jumped out of the car and ran over to him, getting there at the same time as the cops.

"Dad!" she cried.

Grandpa looked up at her like he had never seen her before. He looked very upset and angry. He pointed at his ankle. He said something, but I couldn't hear him from inside the car.

I got out of the car and stood at a distance with Dad. The cops were standing a little closer, and I heard the one radio for an ambulance. Then I saw why.

Grandpa's foot was at an awkward angle and he had fallen in a puddle, which made it look like he had wet his pants. He was crying and then Mom was crying.

"You okay for a minute?" Dad asked me. I nodded, mute. He went over to Mom and the two of them knelt down with Grandpa. Mom took Grandpa's hand. I couldn't hear her, but I could see her whispering things, and eventually Grandpa seemed to calm down.

I felt so dumb and so useless. I crawled into the back seat and closed the door. How could I have thought Grandpa was faking? Who would ever fake this?

Mom and Dad stayed with Grandpa until the sirens of the ambulance were almost on top of us. Then Dad came back to the car. He got into the driver's seat. He had my backpack in his hands. He opened my backpack and pulled out the tablet. "You kind of saved the day with this, buddy."

"Yeah, I guess," I sniffed.

"What else is in here?" He pulled out the envelope for the FBI.

"It's nothing," I mumbled. "It's stupid."

"What is it? The FBI? Is it a school thing?"

"Dad, it's nothing. It's stupid. Give it back," I said, grabbing at the envelope from the back seat but missing it.

"Hey, Cooper, chill out. I just want to know what this is," he said, holding it out of my reach.

I didn't respond.

"All right then," he said. "We can talk about it later." He put my envelope on the dashboard of the truck and handed me my backpack.

Mom came back to the truck, wiping her eyes. She leaned into Dad's open window. "I'm going to go with Dad. Can you meet us at the Delta hospital? They're going to do some X-rays and such." She sighed, and Dad leaned over and kissed her forehead. "I'm ready for this day to be over."

And at the same time, Dad and I responded, "Me too."

CHAPTER 30

We spent a long time at the Delta hospital, although I napped on the hard waiting-room chairs for most of it. We stopped at White Spot on the way home for dinner and ate in a tired silence. Mom didn't even say anything when I ordered a Coke.

It wasn't until after I'd gone to bed that Mom and Dad brought up the case file. They came into my room; Dad was holding the envelope, and I could tell it had been opened. I put my comic down. Dana Scully jumped up, going from person to person, excited by the close quarters of everyone around her. I pulled her into my lap.

"Why did you open it? That was private," I said.

"You're twelve, buddy. Nothing you have is actually private," Dad said.

"Still," I said.

"So, you think your grandpa is the most wanted man in America?" Dad said, changing the subject.

"Maybe. I don't know."

Mom sat down on my bed next to me. "Cooper,

this project . . . it's great. You've done a lot of work, and I love — I really love — how much you've learned about Grandpa in putting it together. And we both love that you have such big ideas. But . . . well, honey, I hate to break it to you, but your grandfather just wasn't that interesting. He moved to Canada to marry Grandma in 1972. I mean, I think it's possible — and I mean, very minorly possible — that he came to Canada as a draft dodger from the Vietnam War, but I don't even think that happened."

"Yeah. I read about draft dodgers, Mom. A bunch of guys who didn't want to fight in the Vietnam War ran away to Canada. But I don't think that was Grandpa. He was in the navy. Why wouldn't he have wanted to go? I think there was something more there. The money. The plane. The . . . the . . . there was other stuff too. I think he had a reason," I explained.

"Buddy, there were, like, twenty, thirty thousand guys who came to Canada as draft dodgers. Don't you think the chances are higher that Don was one of them than this one guy who may or may not still be alive after jumping out of a plane fifty years ago?" Dad asked.

I shrugged noncommittally. "My evidence is pretty tight," I said quietly.

Mom handed back my envelope. "You've put together quite a case, it seems. But I think you should lay off sending it to the FBI. Whether Grandpa is

D.B. Cooper or not, shouldn't we just enjoy having him close by for a little while longer?"

I disagreed. "No! If he goes to Memory Lane, then we won't have any money and you guys will keep fighting and get divorced and I'll have to choose who to live with! He's ruining everything!" I threw my head into my pillow so that I didn't have to look at either Dad or Mom.

They were silent, so I knew I was right.

"You guys can go now. I'm tired," I said into the pillow, but they didn't move.

Mom started. "Cooper, honey."

"Buddy, we aren't getting divorced," Dad interrupted.

"Yeah right. I know you are," I mumbled.

"Things have been a little stressful with your grandfather. It's expensive to have him in a home. But he's also sick, and it makes me sad and frustrated and . . ." Mom stopped talking, but I didn't look up to see why.

"And we're trying to figure things out. And the money thing, that's not something you need to worry about. But we're working it out. I promise you, we're not getting divorced. All of this, it's not anyone's fault. This is kind of what life is like. Sucky sometimes," Dad said.

"But it *is* someone's fault. It's Grandpa's fault," I said.

"Hon, we can't blame Grandpa for getting sick. I know it's hard. Sometimes I blame him too. I want to be mad at him too. But we also love him and care about him and want the best for him," Mom said.

I didn't answer her. I didn't know what to say.

"We're sorry that you were worried about your mom and me. That's not fair to you."

I didn't answer Dad either.

"We love you," Mom said.

I nodded into my pillow. "I know."

I felt a pause from them both, and I couldn't tell if they wanted to say something more or if I was supposed to say something. Then Dad leaned down and kissed the back of my head, and I felt Mom's hand on my back, and then they both said good night. The bed shifted as they stood up and left, closing the door behind them.

It took me a long time to get to sleep that night. I felt caught in a whirlwind of thoughts, going around and around the events of the day. It was hard to believe that Grandpa was just a normal guy who moved to Canada because he fell in love and hated a war. If Grandpa wasn't D.B. Cooper, then who was he? Just a normal, boring guy? That made him just one of the blob people at Memory Lane. I wanted to be angry at someone, but no one was there, so I punched my pillow. It didn't make a difference though. All it did was wake up Dana Scully, who came over and licked my face until I nudged her away.

CHAPTER 31

The next morning I woke up exhausted. I still felt pretty terrible. I asked Mom if I had to go to school.

"Of course you have to go to school," she said, and that was the end of the discussion.

I asked to spend recess in the library, telling Mrs. Berton that I had a headache. I didn't feel like talking to anyone, especially not Tristan, who I knew was going to eventually find me and demand his money. I hid in the library, lying down on the ground between the stacks and staring up at the tree leaves painted on the ceiling, until Ali's face loomed upside down over me.

"What are you doing?" he asked.

"I'm avoiding life," I said.

"Cool." He sat down beside me, so I sat up.

"I owe Tristan a lot of money," I said.

"I know. He said you upped it to two hundred bucks," Ali replied simply.

"I thought it was my grandpa. But it might not be. I don't know. All my evidence is kind of flimsy."

We sat there in silence for a minute.

"What are you going to do?" Ali asked.

I shrugged. "I don't know. I definitely don't have two hundred dollars."

"Tristan's a good guy. Maybe he won't care," Ali suggested.

"I doubt it. You're just saying that because he's your new best friend." I didn't look at him.

Ali shoved my shoulder, hard. "You dummy. You're my best friend."

"Yeah, but you like him better. You hang out with him more."

Ali shoved me again, hard enough that I had to put my hand down on the floor to steady myself. "You're a freak. I like playing soccer, that's why. And I would hang out with both of you at the same time, but Tristan is convinced that you hate him, and I don't want to be in the middle of that."

"I don't hate him!" I protested. "He hates me!"

"No, he doesn't. You always roll your eyes or interrupt him when he's talking."

I started to protest, but stopped.

"You can't even deny it!" Ali kind of laughed.

"I don't hate him. It's just . . . I don't know . . . he's just . . . he's your friend, not mine."

"You could be his friend. He's a weirdo, like us. He even has an antenna thing in his yard to try to pick up alien signals."

I laughed. "That's super weird." And kind of awesome, I thought.

"I showed him an episode of *The X-Files* on the weekend and he loved it."

"Well, duh. It's the best," I said.

Ali got up. "I'm going to play soccer."

"Okay," I said. "I'm going to stay here."

He grabbed my arm and pulled me up. "Dude, you are also coming to play soccer."

I groaned. "Noooo . . ." But I followed him out to the field anyway.

The game was in full force when we got there, so Ali and I had to split up to make the teams even. He ran off, leaving me on Tristan's team. I walked over to Tristan while the ball was at the other end of the field.

"Hey," I said. "Are we winning?"

Tristan nodded. "We sure are." He was watching the play intently.

"Um . . . I know that I owe you money." I pretended to be watching the ball too.

"Oh yeah!" He turned and grinned. "No sign of the skyjacker?"

"I'm still pretty sure I know who it is. I just don't have any concrete evidence." I paused. "But I don't have the money either."

"Who do you think it is?" he asked. "Actually, hold on, I gotta get this." He ran off after the rest of the kids playing, scooping up the ball from under Ali's foot with this amazing flick of his ankle. He took off, pinging the ball off his feet all the way down the field, and then knocked it into the goal.

The team cheered, and he ran back to me, flushed and breathing heavily. He held his hand up, so I gave him a high-five.

"You're really good!" I said.

He smiled modestly. "I just got lucky."

"I don't think so. You're fast."

"I just like running. Anyway . . ." He changed the subject. "About the bet." He paused and my stomach dropped. "Do you have any of the money? See, my dog died this summer and I really want to get another one, but my dad said I could only get one if I paid for it myself. So I'm trying to save up."

"Oh . . ." I thought about Dana Scully and how much I would miss her if she died. "I guess, well, I have some American money." I thought about all the American dollar bills Grandpa had given me. I didn't know the exact number, but I had quite a few.

"Hold on." Tristan ran off to join the game again. Waiting those few moments felt like forever. He almost scored again, but Hazel caught it as it reached the net. Tristan laughed and gave Hazel a thumbs-up from midfield.

"American money is worth, what, like double our money?" he said. "I'd be cool with that, if you are. Let's make a deal? Twenty-five bucks American."

"DEAL!" I shouted. I had to have at least fifty, so that meant I could keep some too.

"I'm not done. Twenty-five bucks American, and you help me with a project at home. Ali said you know stuff about unexplained phenomena. I need your help."

"Oh. Ummm . . . okay, I guess. Yeah. I guess that works."

Tristan's eyes lit up. "Really? Sweet. Okay. Awesome. Maybe you and Ali could come over after school tomorrow. Oh man! Check it! Wipeout!"

Before I could answer, he ran off again into the game, where Ali had slid in a mud puddle. I stood on the sidelines watching. I couldn't decide how I felt. Relief? Annoyance? He and Ali were laughing at something that I missed, and my gut wrenched. But then Tristan pointed to me, and Ali waved me over, so I swallowed hard and ran to the goalpost.

"What's so funny?" I asked.

"Ali looks like he took a dump in his pants!" Tristan was laughing so hard he could barely breathe. Ali spun around to show me the mud stain down his butt.

I laughed too, and after a moment I put my hand up and gave Tristan a high-five.

CHAPTER 32

I hadn't seen Grandpa since he sprained his ankle and was moved into Memory Lane. I just didn't want to go, and Mom didn't make me go with her either. I put my envelope with the D.B. Cooper case file in my desk drawer and left it there.

I mostly hung out with Ali and Tristan when Mom would go; we would take Dana Scully for walks, because Tristan loved her. He always wanted me to bring her to his house when we worked on his alien-antenna invention. He had rigged up a radio system in his backyard to pick up alien signals. Mr. Khoury even let us use his old telephoto lens in case we could get photos of extraterrestrials, but we mostly took up-close photos inside our mouths, which were super hilarious and gross.

A couple of weeks later I came home to find that I had mail. It was a package of books from Mrs. Kim, just like she said she would send. One was all about aliens, so I lent it to Tristan for his project.

The only thing that kind of sucked was that Ali and Tristan had soccer twice a week. I couldn't help but feel jealous about it, but at least Ali never invited Tristan to come over and draw comics with us. I mean, I didn't mind the guy, but I still liked having the American Marmot be just our thing.

Mom and Dad were doing better too. Mom was still picking up lots of extra shifts, and Dad worked on the weekends sometimes, and I would still hear them arguing, but at least they were quieter about it. I overheard Mom telling Marilyn that she had found a podcast on relationship communication that they both listened to. It sounded super lame and boring, but at least they didn't fight as often and they were both home every night. Mom also perked up a lot when we found out Auntie Jane was coming for three weeks at Christmas, even though she grumbled about having to clean the guest room and how her sister never did the dishes.

I kind of felt like Grandpa had died, even though he was actually closer to us than ever. Memory Lane was a fifteen-minute bus ride away. We could have walked there if we wanted to walk up a giant hill on the way home. I felt kind of guilty for not visiting him, but he wouldn't have noticed anyway.

It was almost a month before Mom even asked if I wanted to come with her. It was pouring rain, and the December day was dreary and dark grey. I was lying on my bed reading comics when she came to the door.

"I'm going to see Grandpa," she announced. "Would you like to come?"

"No thanks," I said.

"Fair enough," she said, and turned to leave. "Dad's watching TV. Think of something for supper and make sure Dana Scully gets outside."

"Do you want me to come?" I asked.

Mom stopped. "I want you to come if you want to come. It's totally up to you. I know it can be upsetting to see Grandpa the way he is. I shouldn't have forced you to come the rest of the time. That was more for me than for him or you. I like having you there. It makes it easier, I guess." She smiled.

I put my comic down. "I guess I could come."

"Hon, you really don't have to if you don't want. It can be pretty boring."

"It's pretty boring here too," I said.

"You sure?" she said.

I shrugged. "Sure."

Mom brightened. "I'm glad you're coming. Sometimes there's entertainment on Sundays. It can be fun."

So we went to Memory Lane.

"He probably won't remember you," Mom cautioned as we arrived.

"Yeah, I know," I said.

"It might be weird," she said.

"Okay, Mom."

"We can leave whenever you want to. Just say the word," she said.

Her nervousness was making me nervous, so I put my hand on her sleeve.

"Hey, Mom. Why is Batman so good at basketball?"

"Oh, I don't know. Because he can fly?"

I sighed. "Mom. Batman can't fly."

"He can't?"

"No."

"So then why is he so good at basketball?" she asked, like it was a real question.

"Never mind. The joke's gone now."

It seemed to work though. She laughed a little and punched in the code to the door.

Grandpa was in the lounge with all the other patients, sitting in a semicircle around a makeshift stage with a keyboard in the middle. He was still in a wheelchair because of his sprained ankle, so Mom wheeled him over to the door where I stood.

"Hi, Grandpa. I'm Cooper," I said.

There was no recognition in his face at all. "Hello," he grunted.

"Cooper, grab a couple of those chairs and we can sit together for the concert," Mom said, pointing at the chairs on the side of the room.

I set up the folding chairs beside Grandpa at the back of the room. We sat down, and Mom took Grandpa's hand. He let her do it, but he didn't hold her hand back.

A guy walked over to the keyboard.

"HOWDY! MY NAME'S HERMAN, BUT YOU

CAN CALL ME ANYTHING YOU LIKE. JUST DON'T CALL ME LATE FOR DINNER!" Herman shouted. There was no response from the crowd. "I'M HERE TO PLAY YOU A FEW OLDIES BUT GOODIES. SING ALONG IF YOU KNOW THEM!"

Herman clapped for himself, but no one else did. Then he powered up the keyboard and started singing very loudly.

It was one of the cheesiest things I have ever seen. His facial expressions were so big that it was almost creepy, overextending his mouth and raising his eyebrows up and down while he shouted his song.

"This is terrible!" I leaned over Grandpa to say to my mom. Grandpa snorted in response.

I looked at him. "I'm right, aren't I? This is terrible!" I said to Grandpa.

"THIS IS TERRIBLE!" he yelled. We both laughed, making Herman stutter in his next song, and then he had to restart. Mom shushed us both.

All through the next few songs, Grandpa would turn to me and say "this is terrible," sometimes loudly, sometimes whispering it. I laughed every time. If nothing else, Grandpa remembered to have good taste in music.

We took Grandpa back to his room after the concert, and as we were going into his room I noticed that there were small glass-and-wood boxes beside each door.

"What is that for?" I asked Mom.

"Oh, they're called memory boxes? Something like that. You can put photos or art or knick-knacks in them. I keep meaning to do something for Grandpa, but I haven't gotten to it yet. Do you have any ideas of what we should put in?"

"Maybe. I could help you do it if you want."

Mom smiled. "That would be great."

Then she pulled me in for a hug, which was annoying and embarrassing, so I shrugged her off.

"Bye, Grandpa," I said. "See you next week maybe."

"This is terrible!" he said.

"This is terrible!" I agreed. But it wasn't as bad as I thought.

**

That night I pulled my case file out from under all the stuff in my desk drawer.

I pieced my crime board back together and put it on the floor of my bedroom. I studied it. I did a really good job. In fact, the more I looked at my crime board, the more convinced I was that I was right about Grandpa being D.B. Cooper.

My parents didn't know what they were talking about. Grandpa had a ton of secrets. He was way cooler than they were giving him credit for. And if he couldn't remember that part, then it was my grandsonly duty to do it for him.

CASE: 0024 / FILE: 0011
LOCATION: Vancouver, British Columbia
STATUS: Unsolved

Agent Cooper Arcano has decided that Case File
0024 will remain open for further investigation.
It is uncertain whether the suspect, Bartholomew
D. Cooke, is D.B. Cooper. Evidence suggests that
he is, but due to the suspect's incredible ability
to keep secrets hidden from everyone, including
himself, the case will be put on hold for the time
being and not sent in to the FBI yet.

This is also the addition of a road map of
Washington, marking six potential spots of money
drop-offs for D.B. Cooper's $200,000. Negotiation
with the Parental Unit for a camping road trip
next summer has begun. Requests are being
vehemently denied. For now.

END MISSIVE

ABOUT D.B. COOPER

The story of Cooper Arcano and his grandfather is one that I made up, but the story of D.B. Cooper jumping from a plane is true! It happened a pretty long time ago — on November 24, 1971 — and times were different. There was no security at the airport, for instance. Passengers didn't need identification, like a passport or driver's licence, to board a plane. That's why no one knows who D.B. Cooper was or what he really looked like.

A man calling himself Dan Cooper boarded Flight 305 in Portland, Oregon, headed to Seattle, Washington. After takeoff he called over the flight attendant and told her he had a bomb in his bag. He showed her inside the bag: there were red sticks, wires and a battery, enough to seem like a real bomb — but no one is really sure if it was. He wanted $200,000 in cash and four parachutes. The authorities agreed to his demands, saying they would have the money and the parachutes ready for him in Seattle.

The plane landed and the other passengers got off. The only people left on board were the flight attendant, pilot, co-pilot and Mr. Cooper. The authorities brought on the money, in wads of marked twenty-dollar bills, along with the four parachutes. From there, Mr. Cooper demanded that the pilot fly to Mexico City, but never above 10,000 feet. He had an altimeter, an instrument that would tell him how high they were flying.

Once they levelled out at 10,000 feet, Mr. Cooper

tore open one of the parachutes and stuffed all the money inside it. He put another one on and ordered the flight attendant to close the curtain to first class, go into the cockpit, and lock the door.

Minutes later the cabin pressure changed and a light went on indicating that one of the back doors was open. The pilot then landed the plane in Reno, Nevada. D.B. Cooper was gone.

The only evidence left on the plane was his clip-on tie, which has since been tested for DNA as well as other materials to give the FBI clues as to the identity of D.B. Cooper. The FBI set up a huge manhunt to find him, focusing mostly on Washington and Oregon, where he had jumped out of the plane. He has never been found, although the internet is full of theories as to who he may have been.

The only thing that ever was found was $5,800. It was discovered by an eight-year-old boy. In 1980, nine years after D.B. Cooper had jumped from the plane, Brian Ingram was camping at a place called Tena Bar when he found the money buried on the side of a riverbank. There were two packs of one hundred twenty-dollar bills, and one pack of ninety twenty-dollar bills. The money was positively identified as being bills given to D.B. Cooper. The FBI took some for evidence, and Brian Ingram got to keep some. The remaining $194,200 is still missing.

In 2016 the FBI suspended active investigation into the D.B. Cooper mystery, and the case remains unsolved. So, what do you think happened to D.B. Cooper?

ACKNOWLEDGEMENTS

Thank you so very much to the BC Arts Council for the financial support during the writing of this book.

I wholeheartedly thank the Writers' Trust of Canada for giving me the best three months of my life at the Berton House in Dawson City, Yukon, where I wrote most of *Finding Cooper* and also found my favourite cold-weathered but warm-hearted community. Sadly, I did not find the actual D.B. Cooper, although that wouldn't have surprised me.

A huge thank you to my agent, Hilary McMahon, along with editor Anne Shone, who guided me to take Cooper where he needed to go. Thanks to Erin Haggett, Andrea Casault, Diane Kerner and so many other amazing teammates at Scholastic Canada for bringing this book to life and into readers' hands.

To those who listened to me brainstorm out loud, read early drafts, and gave comments along the way, Jennifer Macleod, Tanya Lloyd Kyi, Rachelle Delaney, Kallie George, Lori Sherritt-Fleming, Christy Goerzen, Maryn Quarless, as well as Jennifer Lin, Stephanie Slen and Piper Yan: thank you. As well, thanks to my family, who are always in my corner.

Geoffrey Gray's *Skyjack* provided plenty of fodder for D.B. Cooper theory-building. And to grandfathers: my own two (one who lived in Ladner and hung out at McDonald's, but was most definitely not a skyjacker) and those I know now. You are legendary.